"Pierce fancies hi...

"Eventually he will come to his sen... Amanda Ralston, a woman chosen for him by his father and myself. Amanda is of a proper New York family and can offer Pierce much by their marriage." Darlene felt as though Eugenia had actually struck her a blow. "You, my dear, simply cannot be so heartless as to want Pierce to give up the things which make him happiest."

"Certainly not."

Eugenia smiled rather stiffly. "I'm glad to hear you say it. Therefore, you will understand when I say also, that you cannot remain in this house. Pierce will continue to be confused by you and I'm afraid that if you remain, his father will have no other choice but to cut him off entirely. This would be a grave tragedy."

"But, I thought, well. . ." Darlene fell silent.

"The kindest thing you can do is to leave as soon as possible. Don't make a scene and don't even say goodbye. I will give you assistance in reaching whatever destination you like."

Tracie J. Peterson is one of **Heartsong Presents'** most popular authors. She makes her home in Kansas with her husband and three children. Tracie has also written eight successful **Heartsong Presents** titles under the name of Janelle Jamison.

HEARTSONG PRESENTS

Books by Janelle Jamison
HP19—A Place to Belong
HP40—Perfect Love
HP47—Tender Journeys
HP56—A Light in the Window
HP63—The Willing Heart
HP71—Destiny's Road
HP88—Beyond Today
HP93—Iditarod Dream

Books by Tracie J. Peterson
HP102—If Given a Choice
HP111—A Kingdom Divided
HP116—The Heart's Calling
HP127—Forever Yours
HP140—Angel's Cause
HP164—Alas My Love
HP182—A Wing and a Prayer
HP186—Wings Like Eagles
HP195—Come Away, My Love
HP200—If Only

Don't miss out on any of our super romances. Write to us at the following address for information on our newest releases and club information.

Heartsong Presents Readers' Service
P.O. Box 719
Uhrichsville, OH 44683

My
Valentine

Tracie J. Peterson

Heartsong Presents

Dedicated to David Brown
with much thanks and gratitude
for the extensive research given
on the Jewish faith, culture, and people.
Bist a mensh!

A note from the Author:
*I love to hear from my readers! You may correspond
with me by writing:*

Tracie J. Peterson
Author Relations
P.O. Box 719
Uhrichsville, OH 44683

ISBN 1-57748-012-0

MY VALENTINE

Cover illustration by Randy Hamlin.

PRINTED IN THE U.S.A.

one

Hear, O Israel: The Lord our God is one Lord.
Deuteronomy 6:4

Darlene Lewy hurried to pull on warm woolen petticoats. It was a frosty, January morning and living so close to the harbor waters of New York City, the Lewy house always seemed to be in a state of perpetual cold. Shivering and slipping a dark blue work dress over her head, Darlene could hear her father in his ritual of morning prayers.

"Shema Israel, Adonai eloheinu Adonai echad," he recited the Hebrew in his heavy German accent.

Darlene embraced the words to her heart. "Hear, O Israel: The Lord our God is one Lord." She smiled. For all of her years on earth she had awakened each morning to the sound of her father's faithful prayers.

Humming to herself, Darlene sat down at her dressing table. Taking up a hairbrush she gave her thick, curly tresses a well-needed brushing, then quickly braided and pinned it into a snug, neat bun on the top of her head. She eyed herself critically in the mirror for any escaping hairs. Dark brown eyes stared back at her from beneath shapely black brows. She was no great beauty. At least not in the eyes of New York's very snobbish social circle. But then again, she wouldn't have been welcomed in that circle, even if she had have been ravishingly beautiful and wealthy to boot. No, the upper crust of New York would never have taken Darlene Lewy into its numbers, because Darlene was a Jewess.

Deciding she made a presentable picture, Darlene hurriedly made her bed and went to the kitchen to stoke up the fire and prepare breakfast. Her kitchen was a sorry little affair, but it served them well. Had her mother lived, perhaps they would have had a nicer house, instead of sharing the three-story building with her father's tailoring shop and sewing rooms. But, had her mother and little brother survived childbirth, fifteen years earlier, Darlene had little doubt they'd still be living in Germany instead of America.

"Neshomeleh," Abraham Lewy said, coming into the room.

Darlene could not remember a time when he had not greeted her with the precious endearment, "my little soul." "Good morning, Tateh, did you sleep well?" She gave him a kiss on his leathery cheek and pulled out a chair for him to sit on.

"It is well with me, and you?"

Darlene laughed. "I'm chilled to the bone, but not to worry. I've stoked up the fire and no doubt by the time we get downstairs to the shop, Hayyim will have the stove fires blazing and ready for the day." Hayyim, her father's assistant, was a local boy of seventeen who had pleaded to learn the tailoring business. And, since Abraham had no sons to carry on his tradition of exquisitely crafted suits, he had quickly taken Hayyim under his wing. Darlene knew that the fact Hayyim's father and mother had died in a recent cholera epidemic had much to do with her father's decision, but in truth, she saw it as an answer to prayer. Her father wasn't getting any younger, and of late he seemed quite frail and sickly.

Darlene brought porridge and bread to the table and waited while her father recited the blessing for bread before dishing up their portions.

"Baruch ata Adonai eloheinu melech ha-olem ha-motzi lechem min ha-Aretz." Praise be Thou, O Lord our God,

King of the universe, Who brings forth bread from the earth. Abraham pulled off a chunk of bread while Darlene spooned cereal into their bowls.

"There will be little time for rest today. Our appointments are many and the work most extensive," he told her.

"I'll take care of all of the book work," she answered as if he didn't already know this. "I've also got Mr. Mitchell's waistcoat buttons to finish putting on. Is he coming today?"

"No, he'll come tomorrow. I told him we must have a week to finish and a week we will have."

Darlene smiled. "Eat, Tateh." The Yiddish word had never been replaced by Papa as she heard many of her neighboring friends call their fathers.

Abraham gave his attention to the food, while Darlene watched him for any telltale signs of sickness. The winter had been hard on her father and even though he'd stayed indoors except for trips to the synagogue on *Shabbes,* "Sabbath" as her American friends would say, Darlene worried that the grip or cholera or some other hideous disease would take him from her.

"You should hire another boy to help you with the work. There's no reason why you should work yourself into the ground," Darlene chided. She had taken on the role of worrier since her mother's death and even though she was only five at the time, Abraham said she filled the role quite adequately.

"Oyb Gott vilt—If God wills," Abraham answered and continued eating. It was his standard response to subjects he didn't wish to continue discussing.

Darlene gave the hint of an unsatisfied snort before clearing her dishes to the sink and returning for her father's. He was a stubborn man, but she loved him more dearly than life itself. She tried not to notice that his hair was now completely white, as was his beard and eyebrows. She tried, too, not to see that his coat hung a little looser around his shoulders and that his complexion had grown sallow. Time was taking its toll on Abraham Lewy.

With breakfast behind them, Darlene hurried to tidy the kitchen. Her father had already gone downstairs to begin his work day and she didn't wish to lag behind and leave him alone. For reasons entirely beyond her understanding, Darlene felt compelled to watch over her father with a jealous regard. Maybe it was just concern over his winter illnesses. Maybe it was the tiniest flicker of fear down deep inside which made her question what might happen if her father died. She had no one else. Even Bubbe, her father's mother, had passed on years ago. If Abraham were to die as well, there would be no one for Darlene to turn to.

Changing her kitchen apron for the one she wore in the shop, Darlene made her way down the rickety wooden stairs. She would not allow her mind to wander into areas of morbidity. She would also say nothing to her father. He would only begin suggesting the names of local men who might make good husbands and Darlene refused to hear anything about such nonsense. She would never leave her beloved Tateh.

"Good morning," Hayyim said with a nod as Darlene passed by.

"Good morning." Her words were rather curt given the fact that her mind was still on the distasteful idea of marriage. Hayyim, three years her junior, was very much taken with her, and looked at her with such longing that it made Darlene uncomfortable. He was a child as far as she was concerned and his feelings were nothing more than a crush. She could only pray that God would forbid such a union.

She was nearly to the front counter when the door bells jingled merrily and two men entered the shop. Their warm breath puffed out against the accompanying cold air and Darlene couldn't help but shiver from the draft.

Dennison Blackwell, followed by his son Pierce, entered

Lewy & Company, stomping their feet at the door. A light snow had started to fall and the evidence left itself on the doormat.

Abraham stepped forward to greet them. "Welcome," he said, his w's sounding like v's. "It is fit only for sitting by the fire, no?"

"Indeed you are right," Dennison Blackwell said, shaking off little flakes of snow from his coat lapel. "It's only just now begun to snow, but the air is cold enough to freeze you to the carriage seats."

"And your driver?" Abraham said, looking past Pierce and out the window. "Would he not want to sit in the kitchen and warm up by the stove?"

"That's kind of you, but we won't be terribly long and Jimson doesn't mind the cold. He's from the north and actually embraces this weather."

Abraham smiled. "Then God did have a purpose for such things."

Dennison laughed. "Yes, I suppose He did at that."

Darlene watched the exchange with little interest. What had captured her attention, however, was the tall, broad-shouldered form of the younger Mr. Blackwell. She stole glances at him from over the ledger counter and nearly blushed to her toes when he looked up and met her stare with a wink and a smile.

"*Oy,*" she muttered under her breath and hurried to lower her eyes back to her work.

"It seems," Dennison was saying, "that both Pierce and I will be required to attend the annual Valentine's ball."

"Ah, this is the auction where bachelors are sold to their dates, no?" Abraham said in a lowered voice that suggested the entire affair was a bit risqué. "Such doings!"

"True enough. Pierce has been abroad for some time and now finds that his wardrobe could use a bit of updating. We'll start with a suit for ball and he can come back later to arrange for other things."

Pierce smiled. "My father highly praises your work. I was going to journey to London and have my suits made there, but perhaps I won't have to travel so far after all."

"Certainly you won't," Abraham said with complete confidence. "We do much better work here. You will be more than happy, I think."

Taking their outer coats, Abraham motioned them into the back room where he and Hayyim would take measurements and suggest materials. Darlene couldn't help but watch the trio as they passed through the curtained doorway. Pierce Blackwell's dark eyes had penetrated her strong facade of indifference and it shook her to the very core of her existence. How could one man affect her in that way? Especially one Gentile man.

She busied herself with the ledger, but her curiosity was getting the better of her. Not knowing what they were talking about was most maddening. If she dusted the shelves near the back room entrance, perhaps she would be able to overhear their conversation. Taking up a dusting rag, she moved methodically through the small room.

"I suppose the easiest way to explain it," Dennison Blackwell said, "is that we too, serve one God, but one God with three very distinctive portions."

Darlene's hand stopped dusting. *What in the world is going on?*

Dennison continued. "We Christians believe in one God, just as you of the Jewish faith believe. However, we believe from Scripture that God has made Himself available to His children in three different ways. He is God our judge, God our Savior, and God our Spiritual leader and consolation. Thus we say, God the Father, the Son, and the Holy Spirit. It's like an apple. You have the core of the fruit where the seeds lay in wait. Next you have the sweet meat of the fruit itself and finally the tough, durable skin which covers over all. One apple, yet three parts."

Darlene nearly dropped her cloth. What kind of *meshugge* "crazy" talk was this? God and apples? Did the Gentiles worship fruit or was that all that existed between their ears for brains? The very idea of comparing God to an apple outraged her. She dusted furiously at the door's edge without seeing her work. Instead, she concentrated on the curtain which separated her from the men.

"Hold up your arm, Mr. Blackwell," her father said authoritatively.

"Please, call me Pierce. My father says you two have become good friends. I'd be honored to consider you the same."

"The honor is mine. Your father is a good man."

Silence seemed to hold the room captive for several minutes and Darlene found herself breathing a sigh of relief. *Good,* she thought, *Tateh won't allow for such blasphemy to continue in his shop.* She was about to turn away when her father's voice caused her to stop.

"So the misunderstanding is that we Jews believe you have taken other gods, while you are telling this old man that there is but one God and you serve Him alone?"

"Correct," Dennison answered and Darlene felt a strange sinking in her heart.

"I remember when I came to America, Reb Lemuel, our rabbi in the old country admonished me to remember the Word of God in Deuteronomy." Abraham began to recite, " 'And it shall be, when the Lord thy God shall have brought thee into the land which he sware unto thy fathers, to Abraham, to Isaac, and to Jacob, to give thee great and goodly cities, which thou buildedst not, And houses full of all good things, which thou filledst not, and wells digged, which though diggedst not, vineyards and olive trees, which though plantedst not; when thou shalt have eaten and be full; Then beware lest thou forget the Lord, which brought thee forth out of the land of Egypt, from the house of bondage. Thou shalt fear the Lord thy God, and serve him, and shalt swear by his name. Ye shall not go after the gods of the people which are round about you.' "

Good for Tateh, Darlene thought as Abraham's recitation ended. He would never fail to tell the truth before man and God.

"There. That should do for you," Abraham said. Darlene could hear the rattling of items and longed to know what was happening. Her father continued, "Perhaps the Scriptures speak not of New York City, but the heart of the matter is still intact, no?"

"I agree," Dennison replied. "And were our God a different one from yours, I would be inclined to agree. But honestly, Abraham, we serve the same God."

Darlene was nearly knocked to the ground by Pierce Blackwell's solid frame coming through the curtain. Gasping, she was stunned by his firm hold on her arm and the look of amusement in his eyes.

"Weren't we talking loud enough for you?" He grinned broadly and released her to stand on her own.

"Shhh," she insisted with a finger to her lips. She moved quickly from the curtain, irritated with both herself for getting caught, and Mr. Pierce Blackwell for doing the catching.

Pierce followed her back to the ledger counter. "I'm certain they would include you in the conversation if you but asked. Would you like to know more about what they were discussing?"

"Leave me be," she said and turned her attention to a column of numbers. She would try for the fourth time to figure out why the column didn't add up to match the one on the opposite page.

Pierce would not leave her be, however. In fact, he made it his particular duty to keep at her for an answer. "I'm serious. My father and your father have been discussing the Christian faith for some time now. They contrast the differences between Jews and Christians and reason together the similarities. I'd be happy to enlighten you. . ."

"I won't hear such blasphemy!" Darlene interrupted. "I won't be *meshummad* to my people."

"Meshummad?"

"A traitor," she replied harshly. "Now, please leave me alone. I have work to do and you mustn't interrupt me again or I shall never find my mistake."

Pierce glanced down at the column of figures. "It's there in the third column. You have a six and it should be an eight."

She looked up at him with wonder written in her expression. His stern expression was softened by a gentle smile. "I don't believe you." She quickly added the numbers and realized he was right. "How did you do that? There are more than fifteen numbers there. How can you just look down at my paper and instantly see that?"

Pierce shrugged. "I've always been able to do that. I guess I'm just good with figures."

"I suppose that would be an understatement," she said, still not allowing herself to really believe him. She tore a piece of brown paper from its roll and jotted down a row of numbers. "Do it again."

Pierce looked at the paper for only a moment. "Three hundred twenty-four."

Darlene turned the paper back around and used a stubby pencil to add up the column. "Three hundred twenty-four," she muttered. She looked up at him with real admiration, momentarily forgetting that she disagreed with his theology. "I must say, that is most impressive."

Pierce gave a tight, brief bow. "So does that mean you aren't mad at me anymore?

Darlene slammed the book shut. "I'm not mad. Now if

you'll excuse me, I have work to do." She hurried across the room and made a pretense of re-rolling a bolt of discarded remnant cloth.

"Well, if we can't discuss religion," Pierce said, following her doggedly across the shop, "perhaps we could speak of something else."

"There is nothing to discuss." She finished with the bolt and took up her sewing basket. "I have work to do."

"That's the third time you've said that," he mused.

She glared at him. "It's true."

"I suppose it is, but does it preclude us having a simple conversation?"

He was so totally insistent that Darlene knew there'd be no dealing with him other than to stop running and allow the discussion. She sat down to her work table and took up needle and thread. "So talk."

Pierce leaned against the wall and crossed his arms casually. He watched her for several moments, making Darlene stick herself twice with the needle. When he said nothing, she finally began the conversation the only way she could think of. "So you are going to the annual Valentine's Ball?"

Pierce grinned. "Yes. My Aunt Eugenia insists I attend. It's for charity and she always manages to purchase my ticket, so I end up with the young woman she desires I keep company with."

Darlene shook her head. "Why not just skip the dance and invite the woman to dinner at your house?"

"My reaction exactly." Pierce laughed. "I told my aunt that fancy dress balls were of no interest to me, but she insists I owe society a debt and that this is one way to repay it."

"Sounds like a lot of nonsense to me."

"Valentine's Day or the dance?"

"Both." Darlene's reply was short and to the point. She picked up a black waistcoat and placed a button against the chalk mark her father had made.

"Have you no interest in dancing or in receiving valentines from your many admirers?"

"I suppose I don't. I'm not very familiar with either one." She stitched the button to the coat and deliberately refused to look up. She was afraid of what Pierce's expression might say. Would he disbelieve her or worse, pity her?

"Valentine's Day can be a great deal of fun. You can set up amusing limericks and post them to a friend, or you can pen something more intimate and romantic and send it to your true love."

"Oy!" At Pierce's mention of true love, Darlene had managed to ram the needle beneath her fingernail. Instantly, she put her finger in her mouth and sucked hard to dispel the pain. Tears welled in her eyes, but still she refused to lift her face.

"Are you all right?" Pierce asked.

"Yes. Yes. I'm fine." She prayed he'd drop the subject or that his father would conclude his business in the back room and both Mr. Blackwells would leave the premises. She studied her finger for a moment then took up her sewing again.

"So, do you have a true love?" he asked.

Darlene barely avoided pricking her finger again. Resigning herself to the path of least pain, she put her sewing down and shook her head. "No. I have no suitors and I've never sent Valentines. I don't find myself in the circle of those who dance at fancy parties either for charity or reasons of romantic inclinations."

"Have you never received a Valentine?"

Pierce asked the question in such a serious tone that Darlene had to look up. He seemed very concerned by this matter, almost as though he'd asked if she'd never had decent food to eat.

"No, we don't celebrate such nonsense. Now, if you'll

please excuse me. . ." She fell silent at the sound of her father's voice.

Dennison and Abraham came through the curtain. "I can have both suits ready in time for the ball. You will be pleased I think, Pierce." Her father beamed a smile first at Pierce and then at her.

"I'm certain I will be, sir." He turned to Darlene once again. "It was a pleasure, Miss Lewy. I've enjoyed our conversation."

Darlene nodded and feeling her face grow flushed, she hurried to lower her gaze back to her work. *Oy, but this day has been a trying one already!*

two

For there is no difference between the Jew and the Greek: for the same Lord over all is rich unto all that call upon him. Romans 10:12

Pierce finished doing up the buttons of his satin waistcoat and went to the mirror. He studied the reverse reflection of his cravat as he tied it neatly into place, then gave himself a quick once-over to make certain nothing was left undone. His gleaming dark eyes only served to remind him of another pair of eyes. Just as dark and far more beautiful behind ebony lashes, Darlene Lewy's eyes were burned into his mind. She had stimulated his thoughts all day, and now as the hearth fires burned brightly for dinner, Pierce had still been unable to put the feisty woman from his mind.

He took up a fine blue frock coat and pulled it on. He adjusted the sleeves and collar, all the while wondering if Darlene would help to sew his new Valentine's suit. It was silly, he knew, to ponder such useless matters, but the lovely girl would not leave his mind, and for the first time in his twenty-six years, Pierce was rather besotted.

Hearing the chimes announce the hour, Pierce made his way to the drawing room where he knew he'd find the rest of his family. Constance, his fifteen-year-old sister, sat rigidly proper in her powder blue silk, while Aunt Eugenia's ever critical gaze roamed over her from head to toe in order to point out some flaw. Dennison stood bored and indifferent at the window.

"Good evening," Pierce said, coming into the room. He walked to his Aunt Eugenia and placed an expected kiss upon each of her heavily powdered cheeks. Then turning to his sister, he winked and stroked her cheek with his hand. "I see we're all very much gathered together."

Dennison turned and nodded with a smile. "There must be a foot of snow out there already."

Pierce shrugged and took a seat on the couch opposite Eugenia. "It's a part of winters in New York. I suppose by now we should just expect it, eh?"

"It makes paying one's obligatory visits very difficult," Eugenia declared. At forty-four she was a woman of proper elegance and grace. Her dark brown hair showed only a hint of gray and was swept up into a high arrangement that made her appear a bit taller than her petite frame could actually boast.

"Perhaps New York society will endure your absence for one day," Pierce suggested with a smile. This made Constance suppress a giggle, but not before Eugenia delivered a scowl of displeasure at her niece.

"Young people today do not understand the obligations of being in the privileged classes. There are rules, both written and unwritten, which simply must be adhered to. It is the responsibility of your elders," she said, looking directly at Constance, "to ensure that your behavior is acceptable and proper."

Pierce rolled his eyes. Aunt Eugenia was stuffy enough for them all. Let her adhere to society's demands and leave the rest of them alone. Changing the subject, Pierce beamed a smile at his sister and asked, "And how did you fill your afternoon, Miss Constance?"

"I wrote thank-you letters," she said with a hint of boredom.

Constance was a delicate young woman. She was just starting to bloom into womanhood with her tiny figure taking on some more girlish curves. Her dark brown curls had been childishly tied up with a bow, but nevertheless,

Pierce saw the makings of great beauty.

"Well, if the lake freezes over properly, we'll go ice skating tomorrow, how about that?" Pierce offered.

Constance's face lit up with excitement, but it was quickly squelched by Eugenia's overbearing declaration. "Certainly not! Constance has been a bit pale of late. I won't have her out there in the elements, only to catch her death."

Pierce looked to his father, the only one really capable of overriding Eugenia. Dennison smiled tolerantly at his sister. "Eugenia, the girl cannot live locked away behind these walls. If she is pale, perhaps it is because her face never sees the light of day. I say let her go and have a good time. Pierce will take proper care of her."

Constance jumped up and threw her arms around her father's neck. "Oh, thank you, Papa!"

"Well, that's settled then," Pierce said with a nod to his aunt. He was growing ever weary of her mettlesome ways and the only reason he continued to endure them was that she hadn't actually caused any real harm. Not yet.

"Dinner is served," remarked a stately butler from the entry door.

"Thank you, Marcus," Eugenia declared.

Dennison came to her side and offered his arm. With a look of cool reserve, Eugenia allowed him to assist her, leaving Pierce to bring Constance.

"Oh, thank you ever so much, Pierce," Constance said, squeezing his arm. "You are a lifesaver. I should have completely perished if I'd had to spend even one more day in this house."

Pierce chuckled. "Well, we couldn't have that."

"What did you do today?" Constance asked innocently. "Did you meet anyone new? Did you have a great argument with anyone?"

"How curious you sound." He led her to her chair at the

dining table. "But the answer is no, I did not argue with anyone and yes, I did meet someone new."

"Oh, do tell me everything!"

"Prayers first." Constance's enthusiasm was halted by her father's declaration.

Grace was said over the meal with a special offer of thanksgiving for their health and safety. With that put aside, dinner was served and a fine, succulent pork roast drew the attention of the Blackwell family.

"So, who did you meet?" Constance questioned, while Pierce cut into a piece of meat.

"I met Father's tailor, Abraham Lewy, and his daughter, Darlene. She's very pretty with black hair and dark eyes like yours. Oh, and they have a man who works for them, but I can't remember his name. He's only a little older than you and quite dashing."

Constance blushed. "Is Darlene my age?"

"No," Pierce replied with a glint in his eye that was not missed by his aunt. "No, she's definitely older. Probably eighteen or so."

"She's twenty," his father declared. "And quite a beauty."

"She's a Jewess," Eugenia said as though it should put an end to the entire discussion.

"That's true enough," Pierce replied, "but Father is correct. She's quite beautiful."

"What's a Jewess?" asked Constance.

"It's a woman of the Jewish faith." Dennison replied.

Eugenia sniffed indignantly. "It means she's not one of us and therefore need not be further discussed at this table."

"Will she go to the Valentine's Ball?" Constance refused to let the matter drop.

Pierce shook his head. "She's never even had a valentine sent to her. Much less danced at a party for such a celebration."

"I should very much like to go to such a dance."

Constance's voice was wistful.

"You've not yet come of age," Eugenia declared. "There are the proprieties to consider and if no one else in this family holds regard for such traditions, then I must be the overseer for all." She sounded as though it might be a tremendous burden, but Pierce knew full well how much Eugenia enjoyed her dramatic role.

"You should ask Miss Lewy to the dance," Constance told her brother. "If she's especially pretty and likeable, you could probably teach her all of the right steps."

Pierce nodded and gave her a conspiratorial wink. "Or, I could just have you teach her. You dance divinely."

Dennison laughed. "Perhaps our Constance could open her own dance school right here."

"Perish the thought!" Eugenia exclaimed. "I have enough trouble trying to manage the child without you putting improper ideas in her head."

Dennison smiled at his children and waved Eugenia off. "It was nothing more than good fun, Sister. Do still your anxious mind or you'll have a fit of the vapors."

Dinner passed in relative silence after that. Eugenia's nose was clearly out of joint and Pierce had little desire to pick up the conversation again if it meant listening to some cold disdain towards Darlene and her kind.

Finally, Eugenia and Constance dismissed themselves to the music room while Pierce and Dennison remained at the table to linger over coffee.

"You seem to have a great deal on your mind."

Pierce looked at his father and nodded. "I keep thinking about the Lewys."

"One Lewy in particular, eh?"

"Perhaps Darlene did capture my attention more than Abraham, but you seemed to have him engrossed with the topic of Christianity."

Dennison pushed back a bit and sighed. "Abraham and

I have been having regular talks about our religious differences."

"How did that get started?"

Dennison looked thoughtful. "His wife died in childbirth fifteen years ago."

"Just like mother?"

"Yes, it was a strange similarity. They were still in Germany and Darlene was only five. Abraham lost both his wife and their new son."

"When did they come to America?"

"Only about five years ago. Tensions seem to follow the Jewish people and for a number of reasons Abraham considered the move a wise one. I believe his choice was God-directed. He worked hard to save enough money to make the move and to set up his shop here in New York. I happened upon his work through a good friend of mine and I've taken my business to him ever since."

"How is it I've never heard you talk about them?"

Dennison smiled. "You've been a very busy man, for one thing. I can't tell you how good it is to have you back from Europe."

Pierce finished his coffee and stared thoughtfully at the cup for a moment. "I've never been at home in New York. I can't explain it. I wasn't at home in London or Paris, either. I guess I know that somewhere out there, there's a place where I will be happy, but stuck in the middle of Aunt Eugenia's social calendar isn't the place for me."

Dennison chuckled. "Nor for me, although my dear sister would believe it so. After your mother died, God rest her soul, Eugenia hounded me to death to remarry. Of course, there was Constance to consider. Such a tiny infant and hardly able to find nourishment in that weak canned milk cook gave her. Hiring a wet nurse was the only thing that saved that girl's life."

"It is a strange connection between us and the Lewys.

Both mothers perished and they lost their baby as well. It must have been very hard on Darlene as well. A five-year-old would have a difficult time understanding the loss. I was eleven and struggled to understand it myself."

"Yes, but you had faith in the resurrection. You knew that your mother loved Christ as her Savior. I think the death of his wife caused Abraham to question his faith rather than find strength in it. When I first met him we discussed things of insignificant value. Darlene was much like Constance, gangly and awkward. All little girl running straight into womanhood. Oh, and very shy. She would scarcely peek her head out to see what her father was doing."

Pierce smiled, trying to image Darlene in the form of Constance. "I'll bet she was just as pretty as she is now."

Dennison looked at his son for a moment. "Don't buy yourself a heartache."

This sobered Pierce instantly. "What are you saying? Surely you don't follow Aunt Eugenia's snobbery because the Lewys are not of our social standing?"

"No, not at all. Social standing means very little if you have no one to love or be loved by. Money has never been something to offer comfort for long." Dennison leaned forward. "No, I'm speaking of the theological difference. You are a Christian, Pierce. You accepted Christ as your Savior at an early age and you've accepted the Bible as God's Holy Word. Darlene doesn't believe like you do, nor will she turn away from the faith of her fathers easily. Marrying a woman who is not of your faith is clearly a mistake. The Bible says to not be unequally yoked with nonbelievers."

"But I wasn't talking marriage," Pierce protested and looked again to his coffee cup.

"Weren't you?" Dennison looked hard at his son and finally Pierce had to meet his father's gaze. "Be reasonable, Pierce. You found yourself attracted to this young woman. Where would you take it from this point? Friendship? I find it hard to believe it would stop there, but there it must stop."

"You've worked to change Abraham's mind. Why can I not work to change Darlene's?"

"I have no problem with you desiring to share your faith with others. But, I think you should seek your heart for the motivation. If this is a personal and selfish thing, you may well cause more harm than good. However, if you truly feel called of God to speak to Darlene, then by all means do so, but leave your emotions out of it."

Pierce tried to shrug off his father's concerns. "You worry too much about me. I know what's right and wrong. I won't throw off my faith or be turned away from God." He got to his feet. "I believe I'll retire for the evening. I have a good book upstairs and I'd like to spend a bit of time in it before I go to bed."

Dennison nodded. "Sleep well, and Pierce, it is good to have you home again."

Pierce smiled. "It's good to be home."

&

Upstairs, comfortably planted in his favorite chair, Pierce picked up his book and opened to the marked page. He was just about to begin the fifth chapter when a knock sounded on his door. By the heavy-handed sound of it, Pierce was certain he'd find Eugenia on the opposite side.

"Come in," he called, sitting up to straighten his robe.

"It's a bit early for bed, isn't it?" Eugenia asked rather haughtily.

"I thought I'd like to read for a while."

"I see. Nevertheless, I've come to express my deep concern about our dinner conversation."

"Concern?" Pierce closed the book and shook his head. "What possible concern could our dinner conversation have given you?"

Eugenia drew back her shoulders and set her expression

of disdain as though it were in granite. "I simply cannot have the scandal of you being indiscreet with that Jewess."

"I beg your pardon?" Pierce felt his ire rise and struggled to keep his temper under control.

"I could clearly read your mind and the interest you held for the Lewy girl. I must forbid it, however. I cannot imagine anything more sordid than you taking up with that . . .that woman."

"Her name is Darlene and she is very pleasant to be around. And whether or not I hold any interest in her is none of your concern." Pierce got to his feet and crossed the room. "Aunt Eugenia, I love you and care a great deal about your comfort, but I am a grown man and I will no longer tolerate your interference in my life. I left this house three years ago because of such discomfort and I will not be driven from it again."

"Well! I've never heard such disrespect in all of my life. I've done nothing but see to your welfare. When my dear husband departed this earthly life, I knew it was my duty to help poor Dennison raise you children properly. If I instilled culture and social awareness in your life, then you will find yourself the better for it and not the worse."

Pierce felt the heat of her stare and refused to back down. "Since you came to me with this matter, I am going to speak freely to you. I am certain Father appreciated the companionship and assistance you offered him with Constance. As you will recall, however, I was already a grown man of twenty-three when you came into this house. I need neither your care nor grooming to make my mark upon society, because I have no such plans for myself or society. These are things of importance to you, but certainly they do not concern me."

"They concern the well-being of this family. Would you see your father's reputation ruined because you chose to marry a Jewess?"

"Why must everyone assume I mean to marry the girl? I've only just met her and I thought she was a lovely creature with a fiery spirit."

"So I'm not the only one to broach this subject, eh? Perhaps I'm not the lunatic you make me out to be." Eugenia's face held a smug regard for her nephew.

"I've never thought you to be a lunatic, Aunt Eugenia. Mettlesome and snobbish, yes, but never a lunatic."

"Well!" It seemed the only thing she could say.

Pierce continued, "I will go to your charity balls and I will allow you to parade me before your society friends. I will use the proper silver and talk the proper talk. I will dance with impeccable skill and dress strictly in fashion, but I will not be dictated to in regards to the woman I will choose as my wife. Is that clear?"

"You have to marry a woman of your standing. To marry beneath your station will do this family a discredit. Then, too, imagine the complications of marrying a pauper. You must marry a woman of means and increase the empire your father has already begun."

Pierce could take no more. He walked to the door and opened it as a signal to his aunt that the conversation was at an end. "I will marry for love, respect, admiration, and attraction, be that woman of Jewish heritage or not. I seem to recall the Word of God saying we are all the same in the eyes of the Lord, and that whosoever shall call upon the name of the Lord will be saved. I realize the importance of marrying a woman who loves God as I do, and if that woman should turn out to be a Jewess who embraces Christianity and recognizes Christ as the true Messiah, I shan't give her social standing or bank account a single thought."

Eugenia stepped into the hall, clearly disturbed by Pierce's strong stand. "You'd do well to remember the things of importance in this world."

"I might say the same for you, Aunt. My father admonishes me to marry a woman of Christian faith, and that is clearly set in Scripture. By what means do you base your beliefs?" He closed the door without allowing her to reply and drew a deep breath. "I've only just met the girl," he muttered to himself, "yet everyone has me married to her already."

three

*And it shall be, if thou do at all forget the Lord thy God,
and walk after other gods, and serve them,
and worship them, I testify against you this day
that ye shall surely perish.* Deuteronomy 8:19

Nearly a week after her encounter with Pierce Blackwell, Darlene felt herself getting back in the routine of her life. She could almost ignore the image of the handsome man when he appeared in her daydreams, but it was at night when he haunted her the most. And in those dreams, Darlene found that she couldn't ignore the feelings he elicited inside her. Never in her life had she given men much thought. Her father urged her to seek her heart on the matter and to find a decent man and settle down. He spoke of wanting grandchildren and such, but Darlene knew that down deep inside he was really worried about her, should something happen to him.

"Tateh," she called, gathering on her coat and warm woolen bonnet. "I'm leaving to go to Esther's."

Abraham peered up from his cutting board. "You should not go out on such a cold day."

"I'll be fine. It's just down the street. You worry too much." She smiled and held up a bundle. "We're making baby clothes for Rachel Bronstein." Her father nodded and gave her a little wave. "I'll be back in time to dish up supper. Don't work too hard."

She hurried out of the building, firmly closing the door which stated "Lewy & Co." behind her. It was a brisk February morning and the skies were a clear, pale blue overhead. The color reminded Darlene of watered silk. Not that she ever had occasion to own anything made from such material, but once she'd seen a gown made of such cloth in a store window.

The sky was a sharp contrast to the muddy mess of the streets below. Gingerly, Darlene picked her way down the street, trying her best to avoid the larger mud holes. The hem of her petticoats and skirt quickly soaked up the muck and mud, but she tried not to fret. No one at Esther's would care because their skirts would be just as messy as hers.

The noises of the street were like music to her ears. Bells ringing in the distance signaled the coming of the charcoal vendor. She'd not be needing him to stop today, and so she only gave him a brief nod when he passed by.

"Fresh milk! Freeeesh milk!" another man called from his wagon. Cans of milk rattled in the wagonbed behind him and Darlene grimaced. She had never gotten used to what she deemed "city milk." It wasn't anywhere near as rich as what she'd been used to in Germany. Rumor had it that dairymen in the city were highly abusive with their animals, and that not only were the conditions unsanitary and unsavory, but the cows were fed on a hideous variety of waste products. Vegetable peelings, whiskey distillery mesh, and ground fish bones were among the things she'd heard were used to feed New York's dairy cows. Even thinking of such a thing made her shudder.

A young boy struggled by with bundles of wood over each shoulder. "Wood, here! Wood!" Behind him another boy labored to entice a mule to bring up the wood-ladened cart.

All around her, the smells of the city and of the working class made Darlene feel a warmth and security that she couldn't explain. She thought of the people who lived in their fine brick houses on Broadway and wondered if they could possibly be as happy as she was. Did fine laces and silks make a home as full of love as she had with her father? *Certainly not,* she mused and jumped back just in time to avoid being run over by a herd of pigs as they were driven down the street.

Let the rich have their silks and laces. Her life with Tateh was sweet and they had all that they needed—the Holy One, blessed be He! But in the back of her mind Darlene remembered her father's conversation with Dennison Blackwell and then her own with Pierce. It was as though another world had suddenly collided with hers. Pierce knew what it was to live in fine luxury. He could have figures in his head with complete ease, and he was more than a little bit handsome.

Esther's tiny house came into view. It was there, tucked between a leather goods shop and a cabinetmaker, and although it was small, it served the old widow well. Trying to scrape the greater portion of mud from her boots, Darlene gave a little knock at the door.

A tiny old woman opened the door. She was dressed in black from head to toe, with nothing but a well-worn white apron to break the severity. Her gray hair was tightly wound into a bun at the back of her neck, leaving her wrinkled face to stand out in stark abandonment. "Ah, Darlene, you have come. Good. Good. I told Rachel and Dvorah you would be here."

"The streets are a mess. If you take my things, I'll leave my boots here at the door."

"Nonsense!" Esther declared. "The floor will sweep. Come inside and sit by the fire. You are nearly frozen." The old woman led her into the sitting room. "See Rachel, our *Hava* has come." *Hava* was Darlene's Hebrew name.

Rachel, looking as though she were in her eleventh month of pregnancy, struggled up from her chair and waddled over to Darlene. Bending as far over as she could to avoid her enormous stomach, Rachel kissed Darlene on each cheek and smiled.

"I was afraid you would be too busy. Hayyim told my husband the shop is near to bursting with customers."

"Yes, the rich *goyim* have come to extend their social season wardrobes. They won't have us at their parties, but they wear our suits!" Darlene said with much sarcasm.

"Who would want to go to a Gentile party, anyway," Esther said, taking Darlene's coat. "You couldn't eat the food."

"Feh! *Kashruth* is such a bother anyway! We'd just as well be rid of it, if you ask me," a dark-headed woman said, entering behind Esther.

"Ah, but what does God say about it, Dvorah?"

Dvorah was much more worldly than the rest of the woman Darlene knew. Her father was a wealthy merchant and could trace back a family history in New York nearly one hundred years. Nevertheless, they were Jewish and no matter how liberally they acted among the Gentiles, they would never be accepted as one of them.

"I leave God's words to my father's mouth," Dvorah replied, swishing her lavender gown with great emphasis. "I'm much busier with other things." She smiled sweetly over her shoulder before picking up her sewing.

"We all know what Dvorah is busy with," Esther said in a disapproving tone. "And I tell you, it is an honest shame to watch a young woman of your upbringing chase after the men the way you do. You need to refrain yourself from acting so forward, Dvorah. Your mother, *oy vey!* What she must go through."

Dvorah shrugged, indifferent to Esther's interfering ways. Darlene saw this as a good opportunity to change the subject. "So, Rachel, how are you feeling?"

By this time Rachel had waddled back to her chair and was even now trying to get comfortable. "I'm fine. Just fine. The baby should come any day and since you've been so good to help me sew, he will have a fine assortment of clothes to wear."

"What 'he'?" Esther questioned. "So sure you are that the child is a male?"

Rachel blushed and Darlene thought she looked perfectly charming. "Shemuel says it will be a boy."

Esther grunted. "Your husband doesn't know everything."

"May God make it so," Darlene proclaimed.

The women worked companionably for several hours and when the hall clock chimed noon, Esther offered them something to eat and drink. They were gathered around the table enjoying a fine stew when Esther brought up the one subject Darlene had hoped to avoid.

"So how is it with your father?"

"He's well, thank you." She slathered fresh butter on bread still warm from Esther's oven and took a bite.

Esther narrowed her eyes and leaned forward. "I've heard it said that he's talking matters of God with the *goyim*."

How Esther managed to know every private detail of everyone's life was beyond Darlene, but she always managed to be right on top of everything. She swallowed hard. "My father has many customers and, of course, they speak on many matters."

Esther looked at Darlene with an expression of pity. "Hayyim said that there are talks of why the Christians believe we are wrong in not accepting their Messiah."

"Hayyim should honor my father's goodness to him and remain silent on matters of gossip." Darlene knew her defense was weak, but what could she say? To admit that her father's conversations concerned her would only fuel Esther's inquisitive nature.

"So has Avròm betrayed the faith of his fathers?" Esther questioned, calling Abraham by his Yiddish name.

"Never!" Darlene declared, overturning her tea cup. It was like all of her worst fears were realized in that statement. Without warning, tears welled in her eyes.

Rachel reached out a hand to pat Darlene lovingly. "There, there," she comforted, "Of course Avrom would not betray our faith."

At this Darlene choked back a sob. "He talks with Mr. Blackwell." It was all she could manage to say, and for some reason it seemed to her that it should be enough.

"It will not bode well, I tell you," Esther commented, refilling Darlene's cup.

Rachel ignored Esther. "Why are you so upset? Has your father said something that causes you to worry?"

Darlene shook her head. "No, but. . .well," she paused, taking time to dry her eyes. "I can't explain it. I just have this feeling that something is changing. I try to tell myself that I'm just imagining it, but I feel so frightened."

"And well you should. If Avrom turns from his faith he will perish," Esther declared.

"Oh, hush with that," Dvorah replied. "Darlene does not need to hear such talk."

"There will be plenty to hear about once word gets around," Esther said rather smugly.

"Yes, and no doubt you will help to see it on its way!" Dvorah's exasperation was apparent. "Leave her be. Come, Darlene, I'll walk you home and the air will cool your face." She got up from the table without waiting for Darlene's reply.

Esther shook her head in disapproval. "You should speak with the cantor, *Hava.*"

Their congregation was too small to support a rabbi and Ruven Singer, a good and godly man, took on the role of cantor for their group. He led the prayers on *Shabbes* and was always available to advise his people regarding God's law.

"Mr. Singer could speak with Avrom, if you're worried," Rachel offered.

Darlene nodded and drew a deep breath to steady her nerves. She accepted her coat from Dvorah who even now was doing up the buttons on a lovely fur-trimmed cape. After enduring another suggestion or two from Esther and a sincere thank you from Rachel for the baby clothes, Darlene followed Dvorah outside.

"That old woman!" Dvorah declared. "Busybody Esther should be her name!"

This made Darlene smile. "She always seems to know exactly what everyone is up to. I don't dare make a wrong move with her only two blocks away."

Dvorah laughed. "She told me my dress was too exciting. Six inches of mud on the hem and she thinks I'm dressing too fine."

"It is lovely." Darlene had thought so from the first moment she'd laid eyes on it, but with Esther, who would dare to say such a thing?

"Thank you. Oh, look, a hack. I'd much rather be driven home than walk." She waved her handbag once and the driver brought the carriage to a stop. "Don't forget what I said." Dvorah waved from the hack and then was gone.

"I won't," Darlene muttered to no one. But already, thoughts of the luncheon conversation were racing through her mind. So much so, in fact, that as Darlene set out to cross the muddy, bottomless street, she didn't see the freight wagon bearing down on her.

Just as she looked up to catch sight of the horses' steaming nostrils, Darlene felt strong arms roughly encircle her and pull her to safety. Gazing up in stunned surprise, she nearly fainted at the serious, almost angry expression on Pierce Blackwell's face.

"Were you trying to get yourself killed?" he asked. Then without waiting for her reply he pulled her against him and asked, "Are you all right? You didn't get hurt, did you?"

"No. I mean yes." She shook her head and sighed. "I'm

fine. You can let me go now." He only tightened his hold and Darlene actually found herself glad that he did. Her legs felt like limp dishrags and she wasn't at all certain that she could have walked on her own accord.

"Let's get you inside and make sure you're all right," he half-carried, half-dragged her the remaining distance to the Lewy & Co. door. Opening it, Pierce thrust her inside and immediately called for her father.

"Mr. Lewy!"

"Don't!" Darlene exclaimed, trying to wrench free from Pierce. "You'll scare him out of ten years of life."

Pierce ignored her complaint. Abraham hurried into the room with a look of concern on his face. His gaze passed first to the man who had called his name and then to the pale face of his daughter.

"What is it? What is wrong?"

"Nothing, Tateh. I'm fine." Darlene hoped that by hurrying such an explanation, her father would breathe easier.

"She was nearly killed by a freighter," Pierce replied. "I believe she was daydreaming and didn't even see him coming. There was no way the poor man could have stopped."

"I'm fine, Tateh. I'm just fine."

Abraham seemed to relax a bit. "You are certain?"

"Absolutely. I wouldn't lie to you." Darlene smiled sweetly, more than a little aware that Pierce watched her intently.

With the moment of crisis in the past, Abraham turned his gaze to Pierce. "You saved my *Havele*. You have my thanks and never ending gratitude."

Pierce looked at him with a blank expression of confusion. *"Havele?"*

"Hava is Hebrew. It means Eve. *Havele* is just a way of saying it a little more intimately. Perhaps you would say, Evie?"

"But I thought, I mean, I remember my father saying

her name is Darlene."

"Don't talk about me as though I'm not here!" Darlene suddenly exclaimed. Gone was the fear from her encounter with the freighter. "My mother liked the name Darlene and that is what I'm called. Now please let me go."

At this, Pierce released her with a beaming smile that unnerved her. He bowed slightly, as if to dismiss the matter, but Abraham would have nothing of it.

"I have no fitting way to reward you," he began, "but I shall make for you six new suits and charge you not one penny."

"Tateh, no!" Darlene declared without thinking of how ungrateful she must sound. She knew full well the cost of six suits and while they were living comfortably at this point, there was no telling what tomorrow could bring. They shouldn't become indebted to this man.

But they were indebted. Pierce Blackwell had saved her life.

It was only then that the gravity of the situation began to sink in. With a new look of wonder and a sensation of confused feelings, Darlene lifted her face to meet Pierce's. "I'm sorry, I just mean that suits hardly seem a proper thanks."

"I completely agree," Pierce replied. "And that is why I must say no. I did not rescue your daughter for a new wardrobe. I have funds aplenty for such things. I happened to be here because I have a fitting appointment. God ordains such intercessory matters, don't you think?"

"I do, indeed," Abraham said and nodded with a smile. "I do, indeed."

His acceptance of Pierce's words only gave Darlene reason to worry anew. It was exactly these matters which had caused her to walk in front of the freighter. Certainly such thoughts could only cause more trouble. What if her father thought Pierce's God was more important and more capable of dealing with matters? What if her father gave himself over to the teachings of the Christians! Esther's words came back to haunt her. *He will perish,* Darlene thought. God would turn His face away from her beloved Tateh and he would surely die.

four

*By faith Abraham, when he was called to go out
into a place which he should after receive
for an inheritance, obeyed; and he went out,
not knowing whither he went.* Hebrews 11:8

❧

Pierce closed the door to Abraham's shop and hailed his driver. He could still feel the rush of blood in his ears and the pounding of his heart when he'd seen Darlene about to die. She'd nearly walked right into the path of that freighter and all with a sad, tragic look on her face. It was almost as if she were facing an executioner. Surely she hadn't intended to kill herself!

Pierce ordered his driver to take him to his commission merchants office, then relaxed back into the plush leather upholstery of the carriage. No, Darlene wouldn't kill herself. There'd be no reason for that. But perhaps there was. Pierce didn't really know her at all. He toyed with several ideas. Perhaps she'd just been rejected by a suitor? No, she'd told him there were no suitors in her life. Perhaps she'd lost the will to live? Pierce was certain she couldn't bear to be parted from her father. Then what had caused such a look of complete dejection?

His Wall Street destination was only a matter of a few blocks away, and before he could give Darlene another thought, his driver was halting alongside the curb. Pierce alighted with some reservations about the meeting to come. His man, Jordan Harper, was quite good at what he did, but Pierce had never gotten used to letting another man run his affairs. Of course, when he'd been abroad it was easy to let someone else take charge. He knew that his father would ultimately oversee anything Harper did, and therefore it honestly didn't appear to compromise matters in Pierce's mind. The only thing he'd ever disagreed on with his father had been the large quantities of western land tracts Pierce had insisted on buying. The land seemed a good risk in Pierce's mind, and it mattered little that hardly anyone had ever heard of the dilapidated Fort Dearborn or the hoped for town of Chicago.

Climbing the stairs, Pierce pulled off his top hat and entered the brokerage offices where Harper worked. A scrawny, middle-aged man of questionable purpose met Pierce almost immediately.

"May I help you, sir?"

Pierce took off his gloves, tossed them into the top hat and handed both to the man. "Pierce Blackwell. I'm here to see Jordan Harper."

"Of course, sir. Won't you come this way?" the man questioned, almost as if waiting for an answer. At Pierce's nod, he whirled on his heels and set off in the direction of the sought-after office.

Black lettering stenciled the glassed portion of the door, declaring "Harper, Komsted, and Regan." The older man opened the door almost hesitantly and announced, "Mr. Blackwell to see Mr. Harper."

The room was rather large, but the collection of books, papers, and other things related to business, seemed to crowd the area back down to size. Three desks were appointed to different corners of the room, while the fourth corner was home to four rather uncomfortable-looking chairs and a heating stove.

Jordan Harper, a man probably only a few years Pierce's senior, jumped up from his chair and motioned to Pierce. "Come in. I've been expecting you." The scrawny man took this as his cue to exit and quietly slipped from the room, taking Pierce's hat and gloves with him.

"Take off your coat. Old Komsted keeps it hot enough to roast chestnuts in here." The man was shorter than Pierce's six foot frame, but only by inches. He ran a hand through his reddish brown hair and grinned. "I've made quite a mess this morning, but never worry, your accounts are in much better shape than my desk."

Pierce smiled. He actually liked this man whom he'd only met twice before. "My banker assures me I have reason to trust you, so the mess is of no difference to me."

Harper laughed. "Good enough. Ah, here it is." He pulled out a thick brown ledger book and opened it where an attached cord marked it.

Pierce settled himself in and listened as Jordan Harper laid out the status of his western properties. "You're making good profits in the blouse factory. They're up to eighty workers now and I found foreign buyers who are ready to pay handsomely for the merchandise. Oh, and that property you hold near Galena, Illinois is absolutely filthy with lead and has netted you a great deal of money. Here are the figures for you to look over. Here," he pointed while Pierce took serious consideration of the situation, "is exactly what the buyer paid and this is what your accounts realized after the overhead costs were met."

"Most impressive," Pierce said, sitting back in his seat. "I see you've earned your keep."

Jordan smiled. "I've benefited greatly by our arrangement, Mr. Blackwell, but you don't know the half of it yet. It was impossible to catch up to you while you were abroad. It seemed every time I sent a packet to you, you'd already moved on. Several of my statements were forwarded, but eventually they'd be rerouted back to New York and, well, they're collecting dust in the files downstairs."

"I kept pretty busy," Pierce commented, "but my father trusted your work, and so I felt there was nothing for me to concern myself with. Of course, I was a little younger and more foolhardy three years ago."

Jordan laughed and added, "And a whole lot poorer."

Pierce raised a brow. "Exactly what are you implying, Mr. Harper?" There was a hint of amusement in his tone.

"I'm not implying one single thing. I want you to look here." Jordan Harper quickly flipped through several pages. "As you will see, I took those tracts of land which you purchased at the Chicago site and in keeping with your suggestion that should prices look good, I should sell as much as two-thirds of the property, I did just that."

Pierce again leaned forward to consider the ledger. At the realization of what met his eyes, Pierce jerked his head up and faced Jordan with a tone of disbelief. "Is this some kind of joke?"

"Not at all. In fact, it's quite serious. I take it from your surprise that you haven't bothered to check on all of your accounts when you were visiting the banks?"

"No, I suppose I didn't concern myself with it," Pierce admitted. "But you're absolutely sure about this?"

"The money is in the bank, and I get at least twenty offers a week to buy the balance of your land in Chicago."

Pierce looked at the figures again. "But if I understand this correctly and I'm certain I do, the original $100,000 investment I made has now netted me over one million dollars?"

"And that's after my commission," Jordan said with a smile.

Pierce shook his head. Who could have imagined such an inflation of land prices? "I knew it would be a valuable investment, but I figured it would be ten or twenty years before I realized it."

"Chicago is bursting at the seams. It's growing up faster than any city I've ever seen the likes of. People are taking packets across the Great Lakes and making their way to Chicago every day. The population has already grown to over three thousand. Why just yesterday I saw an advertisement offering passage from Buffalo to Chicago for twenty-five dollars. Everybody's getting rich from this little town."

"And you saved out the tracts I asked you to?"

"Absolutely! You can sell them tomorrow if you like or build your own place."

"Sounds to me," Pierce said thoughtfully, "that hotels and boarding houses would be greatly in need."

"All those people have to live somewhere, Mr. Blackwell."

Pierce smiled. "Indeed they do."

❧

Hours later, Pierce was still thinking about Chicago. He'd picked up all the information he could find on the small town and while contemplating what his next move should be, wondered if his next move might ought not to be himself.

He left the papers on his bed and went to stand by the window, where heavy green velvet curtains kept out the world. Pulling them back, Pierce thought seriously about leaving all that he knew in New York. It had been easy enough to go abroad. European cities were well-founded and filled with elegance, grace, and fine things. But Chicago was in the middle of nowhere. It hadn't been but three years since the Indian wars had kept the area in an uproar. There was no main road to travel over in order to get to the town, and even packets to Chicago were priced out of the range of the average citizen. Perhaps Pierce could invest in a mode of transportation that would bring that price down. New railroads were springing up everywhere and canals were proposed for the purpose of connecting Lake Michigan to the Mississippi River. It was easy to see that this was a land of opportunity. But could he leave all the comforts of home and travel west?

A light snow was falling again, and with it came images of the young woman he'd held so close earlier in the day.

He liked the way Darlene fit against him. He liked the wide-eyed innocence and the look of wonder that washed over her face when he refused to release her. He liked the smell of her hair, the tone of her voice, even the flash of anger in her dark eyes. He let the curtain fall into place and sighed. If he went west, there would be no Darlene to go with him. At least here he could see her fairly often on the pretense of embellishing his wardrobe. But, a man could own only so many suits of clothing.

He sat down again on the bed and looked at the papers before him. Then without knowing why, he thought of Valentine's Day and the dance. Darlene had declared herself unfamiliar with both, and this had truly surprised Pierce. A thought came to mind and he toyed with it for several minutes before deciding to go ahead with it. He grinned to think of Darlene receiving her first valentine. What would she think of him? Perhaps he could leave it unsigned, but of course, she'd know it was from him.

Deciding it didn't matter, Pierce jumped up and threw on his frock coat. Valentine's Day was a week from Saturday, so there was plenty of time, but Pierce wanted to have just the right card made.

five

*Wherefore the children of Israel shall keep the sabbath
. . .It is a sign between me and the children of Israel
forever: for in six days the Lord made heaven and earth,
and on the seventh day he rested, and was refreshed.*
Exodus 31:16,17

ها

Darlene worked furiously over the cuffs of Pierce Black-well's long-tailed frock coat. It would soon be dark and the Sabbath would be upon them. There was never to be any work on *Shabbes,* for God himself had declared it a day of rest and demanded that His people honor and keep that day for Him.

Esther sat companionably, for once not making her usually busybody statements, but instead helping to put buttons on the satin waistcoat which Pierce would wear the following night. Such deadlines made it necessary for Darlene and Abraham to elicit additional help, and the fact that Valentine's Day came on a Saturday made it absolutely necessary to have everything done as early on Friday as possible.

Shabbes began on Friday evening when it was dark enough for the first stars to be seen in the sky. By that time, all work would have to be completed and put aside. No work was to be done, not even the lighting of fires on such cold, bitter mornings as February in New York could deliver. For this purpose, Abraham paid a *Shabbes goy,* a Gentile boy to come and light fires and lamps. Darlene knew that many families could not afford to pay someone to come in, and for them she felt sorry. They were strictly dependent upon the goodness of neighbors and sometimes they went through *Shabbes* without a warm fire to ward off the cold.

Finishing the cuff, Darlene held up the coat and smiled. She knew Pierce would be handsome in the black, redingote-styled, frock coat. The tapering of the jacket from broad shoulders to narrow waist only made her smile broaden. Pierce would need no corset to keep his figure until control. Of this she was certain.

"Such a look," Esther remarked, staring at Darlene from her work.

Darlene laughed. "I was only trying to imagine what it might be like to dance at a party where men dress so regally."

"*Oy vey!* You should put aside such thoughts. Next, you'll be considering marriage to some rich *goy,* if you could find one who'd have you."

Darlene felt her cheeks flush and instantly dropped the coat back to her lap and threaded her needle. She prayed that Esther wouldn't notice her embarrassment, because just such thoughts had already gone through her mind.

"So, you do think of such things!" Esther showed clear disgust by Darlene's breech of etiquette. "*Bist blint*—are you blind? Such things will only lead you to heartache."

Darlene waved her off. "I'm not blind and I'm not headed to heartache or anything else. I simply wondered what it might be like to own fine things and not be looked down upon by the people in the city. Is that so bad?"

Esther studied her closely for a moment. "There is talk, *Havele.* Talk that should make your father take notice. The cantor knows that Avrom's faith is weakening."

"Never! It's not true!" Darlene shouted the words, not meaning to make such an obvious protest.

"If he turns from God, he will be a traitor to our people. No one will speak to him again. No one of Hebrew faith will do business with him. If that happens, *Havele,* you will come and live with me." She said it as though Darlene would have no choice in the matter.

"I will not leave Tateh. Such talk!" She got up from her work and excused herself to tend to Sabbath preparations upstairs. Hurrying up the rickety backstairs, Darlene couldn't help but be upset by Esther's words. It was true enough that her father would be considered *meshummad*—a traitor, if he accepted the Christian religion of Dennison and Pierce Blackwell. But surely that could not happen. They were God's chosen people, the children of Israel. Surely her father could not disregard this fact.

She finished putting together the *schalet,* a slow-cooking stew that would simmer all night long and be ready to eat for the Sabbath. This would enable her to keep from breaking the day of rest by preparing meals. Turning from this, Darlene set about completing preparations for their evening Sabbath meal. This was always a very elegant dinner with her mother's finest Bavarian china and a delicate lace tablecloth to cover the simple kitchen table.

Setting the table, she hummed to herself and tried to dispel her fears. Surely things weren't as bad as Esther implied. The small roast in the oven gave off a succulent, inviting smell when Darlene peered inside. It would be done in plenty of time for their meal and it was a favorite of her father's. Perhaps this would put him in a good frame of mind and give him cause to remember his faith. Perhaps a perfect *Shabbes* meal would focus his heart back on the teachings of his fathers.

Filling a pot with water and potatoes, Darlene left it to cook on the stove and hurried back to finish the Blackwell suit. Hayyim was to deliver the suits before Sabbath began, and with this thought, Darlene silently wished she could go along to see where Pierce lived. No doubt it was a beautiful brick house with several stories and lovely lace curtains at each and every window. With a sigh, she pushed such incriminating thoughts from her mind and joined Esther.

"It is finished," Esther announced. "I must get home now and make certain things are ready."

"Thank you so much for helping me. Did Tateh pay you already?"

"Yes, I am well rewarded," Esther said, pulling on her heavy coat. Darlene went to help her, but she would have nothing to do with it. "I may be an old woman, but I can still put on my coat."

Good, Darlene thought. *She has already forgotten our conversation and now she will return home and leave me to my dreams.* But it was not to be. Without warning, Esther turned at the door and admonished Darlene.

"You should spend *Shabbes* in prayer and seek God's heart instead of that of the rich *goyim.*"

And you should mind your own business, Darlene thought silently, while outwardly nodding. She did nothing but present herself as the most repentant of chastised children. With head lowered and hands folded, Darlene's appearance put Esther at ease enough to take her leave.

"Gut Shabbos, Hava."

"Good Sabbath to you, Esther."

With Esther gone, Darlene breathed a sigh of relief and called to Hayyim. "The Blackwell suits are finished. You can take them now." She let her fingers linger on Pierce's coat for just a moment before Hayyim took it.

"Darlene, you look very pretty today," Hayyim said, lingering as if he had all the time in the world.

Darlene felt sorry for him. She knew he was terribly taken with her, but her heart couldn't lie and encourage the infatuation. "Thank you, Hayyim. You'd better hurry if you're to get home in time for Sabbath."

Hayyim nodded sadly. Darlene watched him take up the rest of the clothes in a rather dejected manner. Better she make herself clear with him now, than to lead him on and give him reason to hope for a future with her.

Just as she was about to got upstairs and finish with the meal, a knock sounded at the back door. Wondering if Esther had forgotten something, Darlene glanced quickly about the room, then went to open the door.

Five children ranging in age from four to twelve stood barefooted and ragged in the muddy snow. These were her "regulars," as Darlene called them. Destitute children who came routinely on Friday afternoon to beg for food and clothes.

"Ah, I thought perhaps you had forgotten me," she said with a smile. "Come in, come in. Warm yourselves by the fire." She motioned them forward and they hurried to the stove, hands outstretched and faces smiling.

Darlene stuck her head out the door and noted that two older youths, probably in their middle teens, waited not far down the alleyway. She smiled and motioned for them to join in, but they shook their heads and went back to their conversation. They only watched over the little ones. Darlene knew they were probably older siblings who realized the younger children could persuade better charity from sympathetic adults, without being expected to work in return.

She closed the door to the cold and turned to meet the sallow faces and hopeful eyes of the little ones. "I have a surprise for you. I hope you like sweets."

The children nodded with smiling, dirt-ladened faces.

"Good. You wait here and I'll be right back." Darlene hurried into the next room where she had saved them a collection of things all week long.

Nebekhs—the poor things! They had nothing, and no one but each other. Their parents were most likely involved in corrupt things that took them away from wherever they called home. If they had parents. Some were orphans who roamed the streets only protected by the various street row-dies who had taken residence in the area. The hoodlums taught them to steal and to beg and in return, they provided some semblance of a family.

Gathering up armloads of remnant cloth and a small brown bag of sweets, Darlene went back to the children. "I think you'll like this," she said, putting the cloth down and holding out the bag. "There's plenty inside for everyone, even your friends outside."

One little girl, barely wrapped in a tattered coat, reached her hand in first and pulled out a peppermint stick. "Ohhh!" she said, her eyes big as saucers. This was all the encouragement that the others needed. They hurriedly thrust hands inside the sack and came up with sticks of their own.

"Now, here are some nice pieces of cloth which can be made into clothes. And I have a small sack of bread and several jars of jam." Darlene went to retrieve these articles and returned to find five very satisfied children devouring their peppermint.

"Can you carry it all or should I call for your friends?"

"Ain't no friends. Them's my brothers Willy and Sam," one little boy replied.

"Well," Darlene said, opening the door, "would you like for them to come and help?"

"No, ma'am," the oldest boy of the group announced. He had the remains of a black eye still showing against his pale white face. "We can carry it." And this they did. The children each took responsibility for some article with the youngest delegated to carrying the candy sack.

"I'll see you next week," Darlene said and waved to the elusive Willy and Sam. They didn't wave back, but Darlene knew they saw her generosity. How sad they were trudging off in the filthy snow. Little feet making barefoot tracks. Silent reminders of the children's plight. Darlene wanted to cry whenever she saw them. No matter what she did for them it was never enough. Scraps of material and sweets wouldn't provide a roof over their heads and warmth when the night winds blew fierce. *How could God allow such things?* she wondered. How could she?

Without willing it to be there, the image of Pierce Blackwell filled her mind. She wondered if the Blackwells in all their finery and luxury ever considered the poor. The Valentine's ball Pierce and his father would attend was purported to be for charity. Would children like these know the benefits of such a gala event or would the rich simply line their pockets, pay their revelry expenses and advertise for yet another charity ball?

The children had passed from view now and only their footprints in the snow remained to show that they'd ever been there at all. Noting the fading light, Darlene rushed to close the door and get back to her work. There was still so much to do in order to be idle on the Sabbath.

An hour later, Darlene breathed a sigh of relief and brought two braided *Hallah* loaves to the table. Stowing images of the ragged children and Pierce Blackwell away from her mind, Darlene set her thoughts to those of her *Shabbes* duties. She could hear her father puttering in his bedroom and had a keen sense that in spite of her worries, all was well. Taking down long, white candles in ornate silver holders, Darlene placed them on the table and went to the stove. In a small container beside the stove, long slivered pieces of kindling were the perfect means for lighting the *Shabbes* candles. Darlene came to the table with one of these and lighting the candles, blew out the stick. Then with a circular wave of her hands as if pulling in the scent from the candles, she covered her eyes and recited the ritual prayer.

"Baruch ata Adonai, eloheinu melech ha-olam, ahser kiddeshanu bemitzvotav, vetsivianu le'hadlik ner shel

Shabbos—Blessed art thou, Oh Lord, who sanctifies us by His commandments, and commands us to light the Sabbath lights."

six

Wherefore by their fruits ye shall know them.
Matthew 7:20

ᘒ

Pierce lightly fingered the edge of a starfish shell and waited for his name to be called. He hated with all of his being the very fact that he was seated in the City Hotel ballroom, waiting to be auctioned off to the highest bidder. What would happen if Aunt Eugenia failed to top the bidding and buy him out of harm's way? Then again, what if Aunt Eugenia's way was one and the same?

The City Hotel's ballroom had been transformed into a lush underwater world. Heavy blue nets hung overhead to give the illusion of being underwater with a greedy fisherman hovering dangerously overhead. Many considered it pure genius to compare catching an eligible bachelor to amassing a good catch of fish, but Pierce wasn't among their numbers. He was literally checking his pocket watch every fifteen minutes and remained completely bored by the entire event.

"And bachelor number twelve is Pierce Blackwell. Mr. Blackwell, please come forward."

Pierce sighed, adjusted his new coat, and went up to the raised platform where he would be auctioned to the highest bidder. Putting on his most dazzling smile, Pierce pretended to be caught up in the evening's amusements.

"Pierce is with us after a three-year absence in Europe, and the ladies here tonight are no doubt in the best of luck to be a part of this gathering. As you can see, Mr. Blackwell would make an admirable suitor for any eligible young woman." Giggles sounded from the ladies in the audience.

"The bidding will open at one hundred dollars," the speaker began.

A portly matron in the front waved her fan and started the game. Pierce remained fixed with the facade of congeniality plastered on his face. He nodded to each woman with a brilliant smile that he was certain wouldn't betray his anguish.

"The bid is at eight hundred dollars." The crowd oooohed and ahhhed. The heavy-set woman holding the eight hundred dollar bid blushed profusely and fanned herself continuously.

"One thousand dollars," Eugenia Blackwell Morgan announced and a hush fell across the room. She stepped forward in a heavy gown of burgundy brocade. Multiple strands of pearls encircled her throat and in her hand she held an elaborate ivory fan. She cut a handsome figure and appeared to know it full well. Pierce personally knew many men who would love to pay her court—if she was a less intimidating woman.

"The bid has been raised to one thousand dollars. Do I hear one thousand, one hundred?" Silence remained and there was not one movement among the bidding women. Pierce wondered if by prior arrangement, Eugenia had forbid any of them to outbid her.

"Then the bid is concluded at one thousand dollars." Applause filled the air and Pierce bowed low as he knew he was expected to do.

Stepping down from the platform, he went to his aunt and bowed low once again. "Madam," he said in a most formal tone.

"Oh, bother with you," Eugenia said, and swatted him with her fan. "Come along."

Pierce offered his arm and Eugenia took it without a word. Although it was proper for a gentleman to lead a lady, Eugenia clearly made their way through the crowd to

the table she had reserved to be her own. Sitting there waiting was an incredibly beautiful young woman. Her thick
dark hair reminded Pierce of Darlene, but that was where
the similarities ended. The haughty smile, sharply arched
brows, and icy blue eyes of the woman clearly drove the
image of Darlene from his mind.

"Pierce, this is Amanda Ralston. She is the only daughter of Benjamin Ralston."

Pierce bowed before the woman and received her curt
little nod. "Your servant," he said and looked to his aunt
for some clue as to how the game was to be played.

"No doubt you are familiar with her father's name and
their family," Eugenia said with pale tight lips. "I will
leave you two to discuss matters of importance and to
dance the night away."

Inwardly, Pierce groaned. Outwardly, he extended his
arm. "Would you care for some refreshment? The bidding
will no doubt continue for some time."

With a coy, seductive smile, Amanda put her gloved
hand on Pierce's arm. "Perhaps later. Why don't you join
me and tell me about your time in Europe?"

He took the chair opposite her. "What would you like to
know?" He was evasive by nature and with this woman he
felt even more of a need to maintain his privacy.

"You were away a very long time. Did you perhaps lose
your heart to some young Parisian woman?"

Pierce's expression didn't change. "No, I simply had no
reason to return to America."

"No reason? There's a fortune to be made in this country
and men like you are the ones to do the making."

Well, thought Pierce, *she certainly has no trouble putting
her thoughts into words.* "America did fine in my absence."

She laughed a light, stilted laugh. "Mr. Blackwell, you
do amaze me. This is a time of great adventure in America.
A great deal of money is changing hands. Don't you want

to be a part of that?"

"Money changes from my hand all the time," he replied smugly.

"Well, the more important thing is that it returns ten-fold," she fairly purred.

Pierce thought of his land deals in Chicago and wondered if she'd swoon should he be as vulgar as to mention figures. She was clearly a woman looking out for her best interest and as far as Pierce was concerned, her interests were far removed from his.

"I find this conversation rather dull for a party," Pierce finally spoke. "Surely a young woman of your caliber would rather discuss dances and debuts rather than banking ledgers."

Amanda lifted her chin slightly in order to stare down her slender, well-shaped nose. "My father believes the banking system is doomed to fail. What say you to that, Mr. Blackwell?"

Pierce looked at her thoughtfully. She was incredibly beautiful. Maybe too much so. Her emerald green gown was a bit risque for her age, at least by Pierce's standards. Should Constance ever show up in such a gown, he'd be persuaded to throw a wrap about her shoulders. Amanda seemed fully comfortable, if not motivated by, the daring low decolletage of the gown. Her creamy white shoulders glowed in the candlelight, while the ecru lacing of her gown urged his gaze to travel lower. Pierce refused to give in to the temptation and pulled his thoughts away from Amanda. Music was beginning at the far end of the ballroom. No doubt the auction was completed and now the dance could start again.

"Would you care to dance?" Pierce asked politely.

"I suppose it would be expected," Amanda replied.

With the grace of a cat, Pierce was at her side. He helped her from the chair and led her across the room to where other couples were already enjoying the strains of a waltz. Pierce was not entirely certain he wished to waltz with Amanda. It was such a daring dance of holding one's partner close and facing each other for a time of constant consideration. But, he'd been the one to open his mouth and bring her this far. He supposed there was little to do but carry through.

He whirled her into the circling dancers and tried not to think about the way dancing seemed to further expose her figure to his eyes. Didn't she realize how blatantly obvious her assets were being admired by every man in the room?

"Perhaps," he said a bit uncomfortably, "this gown was not intended for such dancing."

Amanda looked at him with complete bewilderment. "Why, whatever do you mean, Mr. Blackwell?"

Pierce coughed, more from nervous energy than the need to clear his throat. "It's just that the cut of your gown seems, well, a bit brief."

Amanda's laughter rang out in a melodious tinkling sound. "Why, Mr. Blackwell, that is the idea."

Pierce felt his face grow flushed. There was no dealing politely with this woman. "Miss Ralston, I am not in the habit of keeping company with women whose sole purpose in designing a gown is that they should overexpose themselves to the world."

"My father says that beautiful things should be admired," she replied curtly. "Do you not think I'm beautiful?"

Pierce wanted to say no, but that would be a lie. "Yes, your countenance is lovely. Your spirit would raise some questions, however."

"My, and what is that supposed to mean? Spirit? Why you sound as though you were some sort of stuffy reverend from the downtown cathedrals."

Pierce turned her a bit too quickly, but he held her fast and she easily recovered the step. "I am a man of God, but not in the sense you suppose. I am of the Christian faith and I believe in women keeping themselves discreetly covered in public."

"Ah, but what about in private?" She tripped and fell against him. Only then did Pierce realize it was deliberate. "Oh my, have I compromised you, Mr. Blackwell?" she asked with a hint of a giggle.

Pierce could stand no more. He set her back at arm's length and admonished her. "If you cannot contain your enthusiasm for the dance, madam, perhaps I should lead you from the floor."

"Remember, you're mine for the evening. Charity and such, you know." She was amused with his discomfort and it registered clearly on her face and in her voice.

Without warning, Pierce pulled her rudely from the circle of dancers. "It seems I've winded myself," he said with a look that challenged her to suggest otherwise. "I'll take you back to our table."

She said nothing as he escorted her back and only after she had been seated did Pierce excuse himself to bring back refreshments. "I won't be a moment," he promised and left her very clearly alone.

Rage coursed through him. She was no better than the women of the night, only she wore expensive satin and jewels. He would throttle Constance if she ever dared to toy with men in such a fashion. Taking up two glasses of punch, Pierce tried to steady his nerves before returning to the table. Without thought he downed both cups before realizing what he'd done. Smiling sheepishly, he put one cup down, offered his for a refill, and picked up another for Amanda.

He walked slowly back to the table. Maybe too slowly for by the time he'd returned there had gathered a number of seemingly unattached young men. He wondered silently if he could just slip away unnoticed, but Amanda hailed him in her bold and open fashion.

"Oh, Pierce, darling," she announced, "I thought I'd simply perish before you returned. You gentlemen will excuse me now, won't you?" She batted her eyes coyly at the group and smiled as though promising each of them something more than she could deliver.

The men graciously but regretfully took their leave, and Pierce was finally able to place the cup of punch on the table at her fingertips. "It was good of them to keep watch over you in case you expired before I returned," he said sarcastically and took his seat.

"Why, Pierce Blackwell, you're jealous." She laughed and took a long sip of her punch.

Pierce couldn't decide the path of least resistance and so said nothing. This only added fuel to Amanda's imagination. "Mrs. Morgan told me that your father is quite anxious to settle you down with a wife. I must say, I was honored to be singled out for such consideration. You know my father has made himself a tidy sum of money, nothing compared to your father, of course." She stopped for a moment, took another sip of punch, and continued, "But together, we would clearly stand as one of New York's wealthiest couples."

"I'm not going to live in New York," Pierce finally announced.

"Oh, well, Paris then? Or perhaps Boston?"

Pierce shook his head. "Chicago." He couldn't help but get satisfaction from the expression of disappointment on her face.

"Chicago? My, but where in the world in that?"

"It's a little town in Illinois. It sits on Lake Michigan."

"And why would you ever plan to live there?" She was obviously filled with horror at such a thought.

Pierce smiled. "Because this is a time of great adventure in America." He used her own words against her, but she didn't seem phased by his strategy.

"Yes, of course, but moving to such a place would be complete foolishness for one of your social standing. Such moves as those are justified by the poorer classes who seek to set up a new life for themselves."

"But I seek such a life for myself. I've grown quite weary of the life I've known here in New York."

Amanda was aghast. "But I could never agree to marry you unless we lived in New York City."

"I never asked you to," Pierce said smugly. "Perhaps my aunt presumed too much. Perhaps she led you to believe a falsehood about me, but I assure you I am no more interested in marrying you than you are in marrying me. Now, I suggest that I deliver you back to your father's protection and end this farce."

Amanda's face betrayed her anger. "No one treats me like this. I am a Ralston!"

"That you are, madam, and if left up to me, that you would remain."

The gasp she made was not very ladylike and certainly louder than polite society would have accepted, had the room been quiet enough in which to hear it. Pierce merely got to his feet, offered his arm once again, and waited for her to make up her mind.

"I haven't all night, Miss Ralston. Come, we'll tell your father that something has prevented my staying out the evening. No harm should be done, as it was Blackwell money which secured me as your companion this evening." With that, Pierce nearly dragged her to her feet.

It was a stunned and openly hostile Amanda which Pierce delivered to the care of her mother. Mrs. Ralston was ever so sorry to learn that Pierce was suddenly called away. Pierce begged their forgiveness, then hurried from the gathering before Aunt Eugenia could spot him and force him to stay.

Outside the hotel, Pierce quickly found his driver and urged him to spare no time in exiting the scene. Cold and uncomfortable in the emptiness of his carriage, Pierce had thoughts for only one thing. One woman. Darlene.

For the first time that evening, he smiled. He thought of how he'd arranged for his valentine to be delivered that afternoon and wondered what Darlene thought of the impulsive and rather brazen gesture. Suddenly he felt warmer. Just the thought of her made him push aside the discomforts of the night. There would be much to answer for tomorrow. His aunt would be unforgiving for his rude escape. But he was much more concerned with how Darlene would react to his card.

His father's warning words came back to haunt him and Pierce was suddenly filled with an uneasiness born of knowing the truth. Darlene was not of his faith and she would reject everything about his Christian beliefs, just as he would reject her disbelief in Christ. Unless God somehow persuaded Darlene to open her heart to the truth of who Jesus really was, further consideration of her could only lead to heartache. But Pierce knew that in many ways it was too late. He was rapidly losing his heart to Darlene, and the thought of rejecting his feelings for her was more than he wanted to deal with.

"She's a good woman, Lord," he prayed aloud in the privacy of the carriage. "She's responsible and considerate, and she loves her father and respects his wishes. She's beautiful, although I don't think she knows it, and I admire her greatly. Surely there's some place for her in my life. Surely there is some way to share with her the Gospel of Christ." But even as Pierce prayed, he knew his words were born out of self-desire.

seven

And he shall be for a sanctuary; but for a stone
of stumbling and for a rock of offence to both
the houses of Israel, for a gin and for a snare
to the inhabitants of Jerusalem. Isaiah 8:14

Darlene looked apprehensively at the envelope in her hands.
It had arrived during the Sabbath and because she knew it
was nothing in regards to keeping the day holy, she had put
it aside until Sabbath had concluded. Now, however, there
was no putting off her curiosity. With breakfast concluded
and her father already occupied with something in his room,
Darlene sat down to the kitchen table and opened the envelope.

The card slid out quite easily and caused Darlene to gasp.
It was cream colored with gold-foil trim and a lace-edged
red heart in the center. The words, *My Valentine,* topped the
card, while at the bottom tiny Cupids held a scroll with a
more personal limerick.

> *My heart I do give and display,*
> *For this, our first Valentine's Day.*
> *Let me say from the start, I will never*
>   *depart,*
> *My heart from yours never will stray.*

Darlene stared at the card for several moments before
turning it over. There was no other word, no signature,
nothing at all to indicate who had sent it. But Darlene was
already certain who had sent it. There was only one possible person. Pierce Blackwell!

After the initial shock wore off, Darlene began to smile. She fingered the lacy heart and wondered if Pierce had ordered this especially made for her. Perhaps it was a standard card he sent to all women, for surely there must be many fine ladies of his acquaintance. A twinge of grief struck her. Perhaps he had sent this as a way of laughing at her. Maybe it was his only means of making sport of her ignorance. She frowned and looked at the card with a more serious eye.

Hearing her father come from his bedroom, Darlene quickly put the card back into its envelope and tucked it in her apron pocket. Glancing up, Darlene was startled to find that Abraham was not dressed in his shop clothes, but in his best suit with hat in hand.

"Tateh?" she questioned. "You are going out?"

Abraham seemed a bit hesitant to discuss the matter. "I am."

Darlene shook her head. "But I don't understand. Is there something we need? Some errand I can help you with?"

"No." He placed his hat on the table and smiled. "I should talk to you about the matter, but it was not my wish to cause you grief."

"What grief?" Now she was getting worried.

Abraham took a seat beside his daughter and reached out to take her hand in his. "I'm going to the Christian church today with Dennison Blackwell and his family."

"What!" Darlene jumped up from her seat, snatching her hand away.

Abraham lowered his head and it was then that Darlene noticed his head was bare. The *yarmulke* which he had religiously worn all of his life, was absent. This was more serious than she'd imagined.

"Tateh, I don't understand." Her voice betrayed her concern.

"I know."

His simple statement was not enough. Darlene came back to the table and sat down. She was stunned beyond words, yet words were the only way to explain her father's decision. He looked so sad, so old, and for the first time Darlene considered that he might die soon. Now he wanted to change religions? After a lifetime of serving God in the faith of his ancestors?

"Why don't you explain and I'll try to be quiet," she suggested.

Abraham looked up at her. His aged face held an expression of sheer anguish. "I've wanted to explain for some time. I know there are rumors among our friends. I know you have had to deal with many questions."

It was true enough. Yesterday, after going to the synagogue with her father, Darlene had found herself surrounded by friends and neighbors, all wanting to know what was going on with her father. Still, she'd not expected such an open showing of defiance. There was no way she could hide the fact that Abraham Lewy was going to the *goy's* church.

When she said nothing, Abraham continued. "There are many questions in my mind about the Christian faith. The Israelites are the chosen people of God, but Dennison showed me scripture in the Bible which makes it hard to deny that Jesus was truly Messiah."

"The Christian Bible is not the Torah," she protested.

"True, but the Scriptures Dennison shared are from Isaiah and those Scriptures are a part of our Bible, as well."

"This is so confusing," Darlene said, feeling as though the wind was being sucked from her lungs. "Are you saying to me that you believe their Jesus is the Messiah we seek?"

"I'm saying that I see the possibilities for such a thing."

Very calmly, Darlene took a deep breath. "How? How can this be? You told me as a child that Jesus was merely a man. You told me the disciples who followed him took his body from the tomb and hid it away in order to support their lies of His resurrection." Her voice raised and the stress of the situation was evident. "You told me the *goyim* served three Gods not one, and now you tell me that Isaiah's words have caused you to see the possibilities of the Christian faith being right and the Jewish faith being wrong?" She felt as though she might start to cry at any moment.

"*Neshomeleh,* do not fret so. You must understand that I do not consider this matter lightly. I am seeking to know the truth."

"But if Jesus is the Messiah, who needs Him? Still our people suffer, for hundreds of years they suffer. Even now, we are misfits, and less than human in the eyes of some. If Jesus is Messiah, where is His Kingdom? Where is our deliverance?" Darlene knew the words sounded bitter, but she didn't care.

Abraham patted her tightly gripped hands. "I only seek the truth. My love for you is such that I would not seek to put your soul in eternal jeopardy. If there is even the slightest possibility that I am wrong, then I wish to learn the right and teach it to my children before my days are finished.

"You see the *mezuzah*?" Abraham looked up to the small ornate box which graced the side of the kitchen door. "Within that box are precious words from Deuteronomy. We kiss our hands and touch the *mezuzah* as a representation of our love and obedience to God's commands."

Darlene looked to the box with its silver scrolling and tiny window. They'd brought this particular mezuzah with them from Germany, and she knew full well it had come from her mother's family. Others were nailed to the wall beside other doors, but this one was very special. The ritual of the *mezuzah* was as automatic and commonplace as breathing. She touched it reflexively whenever she entered the room and because it was so routine, she seldom reflected on the parchment words held within.

"On that paper God speaks saying, 'And these words, which I command thee this day, shall be in thine heart. And thou shalt teach them diligently unto thy children, and shalt talk of them when thou sittest in thine house, and when thou walkest by the way, and when thou liest down, and when thou risest up.' God has commanded me to train you, Darlene. I cannot fail you by ignoring the truth. Should my choices have been wrong, should I be too blind to see, it would be a tragedy. Would you not rather know the truth?"

"But how can you be certain that the truth isn't what you already believe it to be?" she questioned softly.

Abraham gave a heavy sigh. "Because my heart is troubled. There is an emptiness inside that won't be filled. I used to think it was because of your mother's death. I reasoned that she was such an important part of my life, that the void would quite naturally remain until I died. But with time, I realized it was more than this. I felt a yearning that I could not explain away. When Dennison Blackwell began to speak to me of his faith, a little fire ignited inside, and I thought, 'Ah, maybe this is my answer.' "

"But Tateh, how can you be sure? You can't give up your faith and embrace the Christian religion without absolute certainty. How will you find that?"

"Because I don't have to give up my faith in order to embrace Christianity. That is the one thing I continue to come back to. Of course, the Jews believe differently about Messiah, but they still believe in Messiah. To acknowledge that Jesus of Christian salvation is also Messiah seems not so difficult a thing."

Darlene was floored by this and longed to ask her father a million questions, but just then a knock sounded loudly on the door downstairs.

"That will be Dennison," Abraham said, getting to his

feet. He took up his hat and placed his arm on Darlene's shoulder. "Do not grieve or be afraid. God will direct." He paused for a moment. "You could come with me?"

"No!" she exclaimed, then put her hand to her mouth to keep from saying the multitude of things that had suddenly rushed to her mind. Tears flowed from her eyes and a sob broke from her throat when Abraham bent to kiss the top of her head.

He left her, touching the *mezuzah* faithfully, but this time it impacted Darlene in a way she couldn't explain. Suddenly her world seemed completely turned upside down. This Jesus of Christian faith seemed to be at the center of all of her problems. How could she ever be reconciled to her father's new search for truth, when all of her life the truth seemed to be clear? Now, her father would have her question whether their beliefs were accurately perceived.

Her father's absence made the silence of the house and shop unbearable. Darlene had no idea when he might return and all she could do was busy herself with the handwork he'd given her. Hayyim was hard at work in the cutting room when she came to take up her workbasket. He looked up and smiled, but quickly lost his expression of joy and rushed to her side.

"You've been crying. *Vos iz mit dir?*"

She tried to shake her head, but couldn't. "Nothing's the matter. I'm all right."

"No, you're not. You look like something truly awful has happened. Here," he led her to a chair, "sit down and tell me what's wrong."

All Darlene could remember was that Hayyim had shared information from the shop with Esther. Of course, Esther was an old woman, butting in wherever she could in order to learn whatever there was to learn. Still, Hayyim should have been more discriminating.

"I'm fine," she insisted. "There's much to be done and

Tateh won't be back for several hours. He has a meeting with Mr. Blackwell."

"On a Sunday? I thought that rich *goy* went to synagogue, I mean church, on Sunday."

Darlene shrugged. "It is no concern of mine. . .or yours." She narrowed her eyes at Hayyim. "You mustn't talk about my father to other people. There are those who say you gossip like an old woman and I won't have it, do you understand? My father is a good man and I won't have people look down upon him because of loose, idle palaver."

Hayyim looked genuinely sorry for his indiscretion. "Esther has a way of getting it out of you," he said by way of explanation. "I didn't even realize I was talking until I was well into it. I meant no harm."

Darlene pitied him and for a moment she thought he might cry. "I know well Esther's way. Just guard your mouth in the future."

"You know I would never hurt you, Darlene. You know that I would like to speak to your father about us."

"There is no 'us,' Hayyim. I do not wish to marry you and I will not leave Tateh."

"I would never ask you to leave him. I would work here as your husband and make a good life for you and your father. I would care for him in his old age and he would never have to work again."

Darlene smiled because she knew Hayyim was most serious in his devotion. She shook her head. "I could not take you for a husband, Hayyim."

"Because I am poor?" He sounded the question so pathetically.

Darlene touched her hand to his arm. "No, because I do not love you, nor would I ever come to love you."

She left him at that, knowing that he would not want her to see him cry or show weakness. He was still a child in some ways, and although being orphaned by his parents and losing his brothers all to cholera had grown him up, Hayyim was not the strong, intelligent man she would hope to call husband.

A fleeting image of Pierce Blackwell came to mind and Darlene reached into her pocket for the valentine he'd sent. She pulled it from the envelope and for a moment, remembering that Pierce's father was the cause for her heavy heart, thought to throw it in the fire. But she couldn't destroy it. For reasons quite beyond her ability to understand, Darlene put her work aside and went quietly to her bedroom. Going to her clothes chest, she gently lay aside her nightgowns and put the envelope safely away. Replac-ing the gowns, she felt a strange tugging at her heart. Pierce might be a Gentile, but he was considerate and intelligent and very handsome. It was difficult not to be persuaded by such strong visual enticements.

Going back downstairs, Darlene picked up her sewing and began her work. There was much to consider. Her father's words still haunted her and the questions in her mind would not be put aside. Perhaps she would go later and speak with Mr. Singer. Without a rabbi to consult, perhaps Mr. Singer could advise her. But to do so would betray her father's actions and bring about harsh reprisals. Still, to say nothing and have no knowledge of what she should do could only cause more grief. Perhaps if she knew more, she could persuade her father to give up this foolish notion of accepting Christianity as being truth. Otherwise, this issue of Jesus as Messiah was going to be quite a barrier to overcome.

eight

*I know that ye are Abraham's seed; but ye seek
to kill me, because my word hath no place
in you.* John 8:37

꙳

Darlene walked bitterly into spring with a heaviness of heart that would not be dispelled. She listened to her father's words and knew him to be quite excited about the things he was learning. There were phrases he spoke, words which meant something different than they'd ever meant before. Salvation. Redemption. The Holy Spirit. All of these frightened Darlene to the very core of her being.

Now, with less than a week before Passover, Darlene didn't know whether to make preparations for a *seder* meal, or to just plan to spend Passover with Esther. By now, everyone knew that her father was a man torn between two religious views. He went faithfully to the synagogue on Friday evening and Saturday, but on Sunday he went to the Christian church with Dennison Blackwell. He was rapidly viewed as being both crazy and a traitor, and neither representation did him justice as far as Darlene was concerned.

The ringing of the shop doorbells caused Darlene to jump. Nervous these days from a constant barrage of Esther's questions, Darlene had decided that every visitor could possibly represent some form of gossip or challenge related to her father. This time, her assessment couldn't have been more accurate. With a look of pure disdain, Reuven Singer filled the doorway. He wore a broad-rimmed black hat, with a heavy black overcoat that fell to the floor. His long gray beard trailed down from thick, stern lips and one glance into his pale blue eyes caused Darlene to shiver.

"Good morning, Mr. Singer. Tateh is out, but I expect him back soon."

"I know full well that your father is out. I know, too, where he has gone. He's at the church of his Christian friends, no?"

"It's true," Darlene admitted. She felt sick to her stomach and wished she could sit down. "You're welcome to wait for him upstairs. Come, I'll make tea."

"No. Perhaps it is better we talk."

Darlene glanced around her. Hayyim was on the third floor moving bolts of cloth. She knew he'd be busy for some time and would present no interruption for the cantor. "We can sit in here or go in the back."

"The back, then."

She nodded and led the way. Her hands were shaking so violently that she wondered if the cantor was aware of her fear. She offered him the more comfortable of two stuffed chairs and when he had taken his seat, she joined him. Barely sitting on the edge of her chair, Darlene leaned forward, smoothed her skirt of pale blue wool, and waited for Mr. Singer to speak.

"Miss Lewy, it is believed by many that your father has fallen away from the teachings of his fathers. I cannot say how much this grieves and angers me, nor can I stress enough the dangers you face."

Darlene swallowed hard. What should she say? To admit to everything she knew might well see her father ostracized by his own people. Deciding it was better to remain silent and appear the obedient child, Darlene did nothing but look at her folded hands.

"Avrom has feet in two worlds. It cannot remain so. He is a Jew or he is a traitor to his people."

Darlene could not bear to hear him malign her father. Squaring her shoulders, Darlene looked him in the eye. "Mr. Singer, may I ask you a question?"

The old cantor seemed taken aback by her sudden boldness. He nodded, his gray beard bobbing up and down with the motion.

"I've heard it said," she hesitated. She wasn't a scholarly woman and all of the things she was about to say had come straight from her father's mouth. She could only hope to accurately translate the things she'd been told. "I've heard it said," she began again, "that the words of Isaiah make clear the coming of Messiah. The Christians believe Isaiah speaks of Jesus, but we believe it speaks of Israel. Is this true?"

The cantor eyed her quite sternly for a moment. "It is true."

"The Christians also believe that Jesus is not only Messiah, but that He offers salvation to anyone who comes to Him."

"And what salvation would this be?" the cantor questioned. "Would it be salvation from the persecution our people have faced from their kind? Would it restore Israel and Jerusalem back to our people? Salvation from what, I ask?" The deep, resonant voice clearly bore irritation.

"Well. . ." Darlene was now sorry to have brought up the subject. So much of what her father had shared regarding the Christians seemed reasonable, but confusing. "I thought it to mean salvation from death."

"You are of God's chosen people, Miss Lewy. By reason of that you are already saved."

"But the Christians believe. . . ."

"Feh! I care not for what the *goyim* believe. You are responsible for three things. *Tefillah*—prayer. *Teshuvah*—repentance. And *tsedakah*—righteousness. If you do what is right in God's eyes, make your prayers, and turn away from your sins, God will look favorably upon you. The only salvation we seek is for Israel. Why do you suppose we say, 'Next year in Jerusalem'? We mourn the destruction and

loss of our beloved homeland. We long with fervency to
return. Messiah will rebuild Jerusalem and the Holy Temple
and restore his people to their land. The Turks now control
it. Would you have me believe that the Christian Jesus came
to earth but was unable to establish such restoration?"

"I don't know," she answered honestly. "I suppose that
is why I ask."

The cantor seemed to soften a bit. "It might be better if
you were to leave this place. Esther has already told me
there is room for you in her home. She would happily take
you in and keep you."

"Leave my father? How could this be in keeping with the
scriptures to honor him?" Darlene was devastated by the
suggestion.

"He is a traitor to his people if he believes that Jesus is
Messiah. He will be forsaken and there will be no fellowship with him. He will become as one dead to us and you
will be as one orphaned."

Darlene couldn't help but shudder. She thought of the
tiny, homeless children who frequented her doorstep. Would
she be reduced to begging scraps of food and clothing from
the friends and neighbors who would deem her father
unfit—*apostate*—dead? She shuddered again. "I could not
leave Tateh. He isn't well and he might die. He needs me to
care for him."

The old man's harsh demeanor returned. "He will surely
perish if he turns from God. As will you. Will you become
meshummad—traitor to your faith and people? Will you
trample under foot the traditions of your ancestors and
break the heart of your dear, departed mother? If you follow your father into such betrayal, you will leave us no
option but to declare you dead, as well."

Darlene felt shaken and unsure of herself. "I. . .I'm
not. . ."

The cantor got to his feet. "Christians have sought to

destroy us. They treat us as less than human and disregard us, malign us, and even kill our people, all in the name of Christianity. Can you find acceptability in such a faith?" He didn't wait for an answer, but strode proudly from the room.

Darlene sat silently for several moments. She could feel her heart racing and perspiration forming on her brow. Why did such things have to be so consuming? The ringing of the bells caught her attention, and Darlene thought perhaps Mr. Singer had returned. Jumping to her feet, she was surprised to find her father standing in the door. A quick glance at the clock on the wall showed her that more time had passed than she'd been aware of.

"Tateh, you're back!"

Abraham smiled broadly. "That I am and I have news to tell you. Come upstairs and we'll sit together."

Darlene followed her father, wondering what in the world he had to tell her. His countenance was peaceful and his smile seemed to say that all was well, but in her heart Darlene feared that this talk would forever change their lives.

"Let me check on your dinner," she said, barely hearing her own words. She opened the oven to reveal a thick-breasted chicken roasting golden brown. Poking a fork into the center of it, she was satisfied to watch the succulent juices slide down the sides and into the pan.

"Come, dinner will wait," Abraham stated firmly.

Darlene closed the oven and took her place at the table. It was always here that they shared important matters. It was at a similar table in Germany that her father had told her of her mother and brother's death. It was at that same table he had announced their departure for America. What could he possibly wish to share with her now?

"What is it, Tateh?"

Abraham smiled. "I have invited the Blackwells to share Passover with us."

Passover? Her heart gave a sudden lurch. If Tateh was considering Passover, perhaps things weren't as bad as she supposed. But to invite the Blackwells to their *seder* was a shock.

"You've asked them here? For our *seder*?"

"Yes. The message this morning at their church was all about Easter and the last supper of Jesus Christ. The last supper was a celebration of Passover. Pierce said that he wondered what that Passover feast might have been like, and I told him he should come see for himself."

"And they accepted?"

"Dennison and Pierce did. Mrs. Morgan, Dennison's widowed sister, declined interest. I don't think she much cares for our kind." His words were given in a rather sorrowful manner. "Of course, she also takes a strong stand where Dennison's youngest child is concerned and refused for both herself and Constance Blackwell."

"I see." Darlene felt a lump form in her throat. "Well, I suppose I have preparations to see to."

"You are unhappy with this?" Abraham looked at her so tenderly that Darlene couldn't distance herself from him.

"No, not really." She considered telling him about the cantor, but decided against it. "I'm just surprised that they would want to come."

Abraham chuckled. "I think Pierce would make any excuse to come. He seems most anxious to see you again. He always asks about you and wonders how it is that you are ever away when he comes for fittings."

Darlene blushed, feeling her cheeks grow very hot. She thought no one had noticed her purposeful absences. "I suppose it is because I have much to do."

Abraham laughed even more at her feeble attempt to disguise the truth. "Daughter, you are not so very good at telling falsehoods. I've seen the way your face lights up when I speak of him. Perhaps you have a place in your heart for him?"

"No!" Darlene declared a bit too enthusiastically. "He's not of our faith and besides, I would never leave you."

"You will one day. It is important for a woman to marry and I will see you safely settled into a marriage of love and security before I die. So, if you think you can prolong my life on earth by simply refusing to marry, think again."

Darlene saw the glint of amusement in his eyes. She loved this man more than any other human being. Falling to her knees, she threw her arms around his waist and with her head on his lap began to cry. "I love you, Tateh, please do not jest about your death. I'm afraid when I think of you dying and leaving me behind. I think of how much it hurt to lose my mother and I can't bear the thought of your passing."

Abraham stroked her hair and tried to reassure her. "That is why the truth is important to me, Darlene. I want to be absolutely sure of my eternity. Does that sound like a foolish old man who is afraid to die?"

"Of course not!" she declared, raising her gaze to meet her father's eyes.

"Well, it's the truth. I am a foolish old man and I'm afraid to die. Dennison Blackwell isn't afraid to end his life on earth because he has great confidence in what will happen to him after his earthly life is completed."

"And you don't have such faith in your beliefs?" She dried her eyes with the back of her sleeve and waited for his answer.

He gently touched her cheek with his aged fingers. "If I could say yes, I would and put your mind forever at ease. But I cannot say yes."

"I'm afraid, Tateh."

"I know." He smiled sympathetically. "I suppose it would do little good to tell you not to be afraid."

"Very little good," she said with a hint of a smile on her

lips. She got to her feet and Abraham stood too, wrapping her in his arms.

"You will make for the Blackwells a fine *seder*?" he questioned softly.

"Of course, Tateh. It will be the very best."

"Good. Now, I must go to work and earn for us the money for such a feast."

Darlene let him go without another word. She made her way to her bedroom and closed the door quietly behind her. Standing there in the stark, simple room, Darlene couldn't help but wonder where the future would take them. Surely if her father converted to Christianity, they'd find it impossible to remain in the neighborhood. Mr. Singer had already made it clear that they would be cut off from the community and called dead.

Drawing a deep breath, Darlene went to her bed and sat down. *No matter what happens,* she thought, *no matter where I am led, I will not forsake my father. I will not be blinded by the prejudice and stupidity of my own people.* She saw her reflection in the dresser mirror and tried hard to smile. Her eyes were still red-rimmed from crying and her face rather ashen from the shocks of the day, but deep inside, Darlene knew that her spirit thrived and that her heart was complete and whole. She would not be defeated by these things. She had trusted her father all of her life. To deny his ability to look out for her very best interests now would be to subject all of his ways to speculative guesses.

Dropping her gaze, Darlene caught sight of the chest where Pierce's valentine lay hidden away. She'd never spoken to him of the matter. In fact, her father was quite right to mention her disappearances when Pierce was scheduled to arrive in the shop. She felt nervous and jittery inside whenever she thought about Pierce Blackwell. There was no future with him, but he stirred her imagination in a way that could be quite maddening. With very little thought, she went to the chest and retrieved the pristine card.

She traced the letters, *My Valentine* and wondered if Pierce had ever given it a single thought after having it delivered to her. He must think her terribly rude to have never thanked him for his thoughtfulness. And she truly believed that the act had been inspired by thoughtfulness and not because Pierce wanted to mock her inexperience with the day.

And now they were coming for Passover.

Pierce and his father would arrive to share her favorite celebration. Would they mock her faith, or would they understand and cherish it as she did? She thought of the recited words of the Passover dinner. The questions which were always asked and the responses which were always given. "What makes this night different," she whispered and replaced the valentine in the chest. And indeed, she couldn't help but know that this night would be most different from all the others she had known.

nine

And it shall come to pass, when your children shall
say unto you, What mean ye by this service? That ye
shall say, It is the sacrifice of the Lord's passover,
who passed over the houses of the children of Israel
in Egypt, when he smote the Egyptians, and
delivered our houses. And the people bowed
the head and worshipped. Exodus 12:26, 27

Darlene had worked diligently to rid the house and shop of any crumb of leaven. She swept the place from the top floor down and burned every bit until she was satisfied that the house was clean. This was in keeping with the teachings of her Jewish faith, and it made her proud to be such an important part of Passover. She remembered asking her bubbe why they had to eat unleavened bread and why the house had to be kept so clean of crumbs. Bubbe had told her the story of Israel's deliverance out of Egypt and it came to be a story she remembered well, for it was retold with every Passover celebration.

"When our people were in Egypt," Bubbe had said, "they were slaves to the Pharaoh. They suffered great miseries and God took pity upon them and sent out Moses to appeal to Pharaoh to let God's people go. But of course, Pharaoh was a stubborn man and he endured many plagues and sufferings upon his own people before finally agreeing to let the Israelites go free. The last of these great plagues was the most horrible of all. God told Moses he would take the life of every firstborn in the land of Egypt. Our people smeared blood over the doors and windows and the destroyer passed over, seeing this as a symbol of obedience

78

unto God. Then, they had to rise up with haste to make the great journey to freedom. There was no time for the bread to rise and so they ate unleavened bread. Thus Passover became the Feast of Unleavened Bread."

Darlene still shuddered to think of such a monumental judgment upon the land. She remembered the verses Bubbe had quoted. "For I will pass through the land of Egypt this night, and will smite all the firstborn in the land of Egypt, both man and beast; and against all the gods of Egypt I will execute judgment: I am the Lord."

Darlene felt a deep sense of awe in that statement. It was such a moving reminder. "I am the Lord." *Baruch Ha-Shem,* she thought. *Blessed is the Name.*

With her mind focused on the preparations for Passover, Darlene forgot about the Blackwells. Instead, she wondered if her father would participate with the same enthusiasm he had once held for the ceremony. Surely he still felt the same about the deliverance of God's people from bondage. Freedom was a most cherished thing in the Lewy household and Darlene knew full well that her father didn't take such matters lightly. But perhaps the Christians in their faith were not so concerned with such things. What if the Blackwells had convinced her father that such freedom and remembrances were unimportant?

This was her first conscious thoughts of Pierce and his father. She grew nervous trying to imagine them at the *seder* table. Would they wear *yarmulkes?* Would they recite the prayers? Would they scoff and laugh at the faith of her people?

Somehow, Darlene couldn't imagine Pierce or his father being so cruel, but she reminded herself that she really didn't know either one all that well. Putting aside her worries, Darlene began to think about Pierce. She'd caught a glimpse of him leaving the shop one day and couldn't help but notice the way her heart beat faster at the very sight of him. Why did he have to affect her in such a way? Why could she not forget his smiling face and warm brown eyes? Sometimes it hurt so much to imagine what life with Pierce might be like. She knew what it felt like to be held securely in his arms. Would he hold her in that same possessive way if they were married? Would his smile be as sweet and his manners as gentle if she were his wife?

"No!" she exclaimed, putting her hands to her head as if to squeeze out such thoughts. It was sheer madness to imagine such things. Pierce was a Christian and she was a Jew. There was no possibility of the two coming together as one.

&

The Blackwell carriage drew up to the shop of Abraham Lewy. Pierce felt the anticipation of seeing Darlene mount within him and he found himself anxious to push the evening forward. If his father sensed this, he said nothing. In fact, little talk had been exchanged between them because two hours earlier, Pierce had announced his desire to move to Chicago. Dennison hadn't taken the news very well. A number of protests to such an idea were easily put forth, but Pierce had answers for all of his father's concerns. Hadn't they been his own concerns when first the thought of such a trip had come to mind? How will you live? How will you travel there? How will you survive in the wilds of Illinois? They were legitimate questions and Pierce couldn't pretend that he had all of the answers.

Seeing his father's brooding face, Pierce offered him a word of consolation. "Don't fret about this which hasn't come to pass. I promise I won't make any rash decisions, and I will discuss everything with you first."

"Discuss, but not necessarily heed my advise," Dennison muttered.

Pierce realized that nothing he said would offer comfort and gave up. He sprang from the carriage and without waiting for his father, went to knock on the shop door. Closed for Passover, the window shade on the door had been pulled and even the shop windows were shaded for privacy. As his father came to stand beside him, Pierce couldn't help but feel the racing of his heart and wondered if his father would make some comment about the inappropriateness of Pierce's interest in Darlene. But before any word could be exchanged, Abraham Lewy opened the door and smiled.

"Ah, you have come. *Shalom.*"

"*Shalom,* my friend," Dennison replied. "And, my thanks for this invitation to your home and celebration."

It was a most somber occasion, and yet Pierce could hardly contain himself. He knew that just up those wooden stairs, Darlene would be scurrying around to make everything perfect for the occasion. He wanted to see her more than anything, and all other thoughts were wasted on him.

"Come, my Darlene has already made ready our table," Abraham said. "Oh, and here." He pulled out two *yarmulkes* and handed them to Dennison and Pierce. "You will not mind wearing a headcovering for prayer, will you?"

"Of course not," Dennison announced and promptly placed the *yarmulke* on his head.

Pierce held the small black piece for a moment and smiled. "My pleasure," he announced, putting it into place. All he could think of was that this might in some way bring about Darlene's approval. He certainly didn't believe it necessary for prayer, but he knew it was something she would expect.

They made their way up the stairs, slowly following Abraham's aged form. Pierce felt the *yarmulke* slip off his head just in time to replace it. Dennison was having no better luck. As they entered the dining area, Pierce saw Abraham touch his hand to his lips and then touch a small metal box at the inside of the door. He pondered this for a moment, wondering what the box represented, but then

Darlene appeared, and he thought of nothing else for a very long time.

She was lovely, just as he'd remembered her. She wore a beautiful gown of amber satin and lace, and her hair had been left down to cascade in curls below her shoulders. Her response was friendly and open, but Pierce saw a light in her eyes when she met his gaze and it caused a surge of energy to flow through him.

"Good evening, my dear," Dennison said first. "Thank you for the invitation to share such an important celebration with you." The *yarmulke* slid off his head and onto the floor. Dennison laughed and bent over to pick it up, just as Pierce's did the same.

Everyone laughed, but it was Abraham who spoke, "For you, Darlene could fetch some hat pins?"

They all laughed again and Pierce and Dennison replaced the *yarmulkes*.

Then it was Pierce who spoke. He tried to steady his nerves and keep his voice even. "Darlene, it's wonderful to see you again. I see you've managed to avoid the freighters."

She blushed as he knew she would at the reminder of their last meeting. "Good evening, Mr. Blackwell," she said rather shyly.

"Nonsense, my name is Pierce. You must use it and give me the honor of addressing you by your given name."

Darlene looked hesitantly at her father and Dennison Blackwell before nodding. "Very well, Pierce."

She hurried away after that and Pierce wished that he could follow her. "Do you need help with anything?" he called after her.

"No. Everything is ready."

She was only a few feet away, but space seemed to represent an unbreakable wall to Pierce. Her rejection of his help left him with nothing to do but listen to the conversation of his father and Abraham, and to make an occasional comment when asked for one.

"Come," Abraham said, "we'll begin our *seder*."

Pierce took in every detail of the setting. A beautiful lacy cloth lay over the table and two lighted candles, in intricate silver holders, were placed atop this. There was also a strange tray of some sort with six circular indentions. Each indention held some food article, but none held the same appeal as the delicious aroma of whatever Darlene had in the oven. Pulling out a chair, Pierce saw that there was a cushion on it. Gazing around he noted a cushion at the back of every chair. Perhaps the Lewys feared that their guests would expect luxury.

Darlene took her seat opposite Pierce, looking up for a moment to meet his gaze. He smiled, hoping that it would both charm and relax her. She seemed tense in his presence and he wondered if perhaps she would have rather he not share her Passover *seder.*

Abraham began the opening prayer and from there the ceremony seemed to pass in a blur of fascination for Pierce. It was all so different from anything he'd ever known, yet there was also an air of familiarity. Had he not been taught from the Bible about Moses and the slavery of Israel? Yet for Darlene and Abraham, there seemed an appreciation for this remembrance that Pierce had no understanding of. He had known an easy life. He had known a life of privilege. Thinking this, Abraham's next words caught Pierce's attention and seared a place in his heart.

". . .We speak this evening of other tyrants and other tyrannies as well. We speak of the tyranny of poverty and the tyranny of privation, of the tyranny of wealth and the tyranny of war, of the tyranny of power and the tyranny of despair, of the tyranny of disease and the tyranny of time, of the tyranny of ignorance and the tyranny of color. To all these tyrannies do we address ourselves this evening. Passover brands them all as abominations in the sight of God."

Abominations in the sight of God? Pierce could only wonder at the meaning for surely God had no problem with wealth and prosperity. Unless, of course, it led to greed and cruelty. He thought of Amanda Ralston. The tyranny of ignorance and color gave him thoughts of Eugenia and her fierce dislike of the Jews in their city. All the things named as tyrannies were the very essences of those things which separated one people from another.

The ceremony continued and Pierce was surprised when Darlene got up and retrieved a pitcher of water, a bowl, and a towel. Abraham noted his confusion and smiled.

"It is recorded in the *Talmud,* the hands should be washed before dipping food."

Pierce watched as Darlene placed the bowl at her father's side. He held his hands over the bowl and she poured a small amount of water from the pitcher. Abraham rubbed his hands together and accepted a towel from Darlene on which to dry them. This process was repeated for Dennison, and finally for Pierce. He sensed her anxiety and nervousness. Without looking up, he held his hands as he'd seen the others do and when she handed him the towel, their fingers touched for just a moment. He heard her draw in her breath quickly and kept his face lowered. Such a sobering ceremony deserved his respect, but he really felt like smiling because he was growing ever more certain that Darlene felt something powerful for him.

After washing her own hands, Darlene retook her place and the *seder* continued. There was a passing of raw parsley which was used to dip in salt water and Abraham directed them all in the recitation of the blessing, first in Hebrew and then in English.

"Praised be Thou, O Lord our God, King of the universe, Who created the fruit of the earth."

There were more prayers and the breaking of the unleavened bread, or *matza* as Abraham called it, and Pierce was completely mesmerized by the process of this ceremony. There were symbolic reasons for everything and he suddenly found that he wanted to understand it all at once.

Without warning, Darlene spoke in a soft, but clear voice that reminded Pierce of a little girl. "Why is this night different from all other nights?"

He wondered if this was part of the ceremony or just a reflective thought because of his presence at her *seder.* He didn't have long to wait before realizing that this was yet another portion of recitations. Abraham spoke out in his deep authoritative voice.

"In what way do you find this night different?"

"In four ways," Darlene answered, "do I find it different."

"What is the first difference?"

Pierce paid close attention as Darlene replied. "It differs in that on all other nights we eat bread or *matza,* while on this night we eat only *matza.*"

"And what is the second difference?

"It differs in that on all other nights we eat vegetables and herbs of all kinds, while on this night we must eat bitter herbs."

Abraham nodded. "And what is the third difference between this night and all other nights?"

"It differs in that on all other nights we do not dip vegetables even once, while on this night we dip them twice."

"And what is the fourth difference?"

"It differs in that on all other nights we eat in an upright or a reclining position, while on this night we recline at the table."

Pierce began to realize the purpose for the cushion at his back. There was so much that he was unaware of and he felt like an outsider intruding on something very precious.

"The four differences," Abraham concluded, "that you have called to our attention are important and significant. They are reminders that freedom and liberty are cherished values not to be taken for granted."

The words touched Pierce as Abraham continued to explain. "To appreciate what it means to be free we must be reminded of how it feels to be enslaved."

Pierce felt a chill run up his spine. He took his freedom for granted. He took his wealth and the privileges he enjoyed for granted. He didn't know what it was to be enslaved, with the possible exception of the way Darlene had enslaved his heart.

Abraham continued with a recitation of the enslavement of the Israelites under the Egyptian taskmasters. He stressed the importance of retelling the story of deliverance lest any man forget God's blessings and the importance of freedom. There were other stories and a remembrance of the ten plagues God had brought upon Egypt when Pharaoh would not let the children of Israel go.

Then came another phase of the *seder* and Abraham raised a bone which lay upon the *seder* tray. This was symbolic of the *paschal* lamb which was eaten on Passover eve when the Temple stood in Jerusalem. "What does this bone remind us, and what does it teach us?" Abraham questioned and then continued. "It reminds us of the tenth plague in Egypt, when all the firstborn of the Egyptians were struck down. It reminds us of the salvation of the Israelites whose homes were spared. For *Pesach* means more than *paschal* lamb; it has another meaning. It means, 'He skipped over.' The Lord skipped over the houses of those whose doorposts bore the blood of the lamb." Abraham lowered the bone and said very seriously. "The willingness to sacrifice is the prelude to freedom."

Pierce felt a trembling in his body and clearly knew the hand of God was upon him. Perhaps he was in more bondage than he knew. He wondered if he had a heart for sacrifice and whether he could give up all that he loved, for the sake of freedom in God.

Abraham then raised the *matza.* "This *matza* that we eat reminds us of the haste with which the Israelites fled from Egypt. The dough that they were baking on the hot rocks of the Egyptian fields was removed before it could leaven, and so it remained flat."

He lowered this and picked up the *maror,* bitter herbs represented here by horseradish. "The bitter herbs symbolize the bitter lot of the Israelites who were enslaved in Egypt. *Pesach, matza,* and *maror* are the symbolic expressions that represent freedom in all ages. Today we might say they symbolize sacrifice, preparedness, and hope. These are necessary elements in the fight for freedom."

Pierce's thoughts were turned inward as the *seder* concluded. He barely heard the words while going through the motions of the ceremony. His heart and conscience were pricked with the meanings and representation of the things he did. When he'd agreed to come to the *seder,* Pierce had thought nothing of how it might affect him. He'd only thought of Darlene and how she might affect him. But now, in the humble quiet of their home, Pierce's mind ran in a multitude of directions. To have freedom from the greed and prejudice of New York society, he would have to sacrifice his comfort. To go forward in a positive and clearly mapped-out manner would require preparation. And, to serve God more directly and in a completely life-changing way would require hope. Hope in that which he could not see, but was certain existed.

The *seder* meal was completed and the symbols cleared away by Abraham, while Darlene brought out a most extensive feast. Pierce watched her intently, wondering quietly to himself whether she'd ever consider leaving New York as his wife.

As they sat around the table enjoying a huge beef roast, Pierce was surprised when Abraham spoke. "Your celebration of Easter seems to share something with our Passover."

"It shares a great deal," Dennison replied. "We remember that Jesus ate the Passover *seder* with His disciples before going to His death on the cross. This time of year reminds us, too, of freedom. We Christians have freedom from eternal death because of Christ's sacrifice on the cross. He prepared a way for us to be reconciled with God, and because of this we have hope that He will come again for us."

Darlene's expression seemed to change from indifference to revelation. She said nothing, but Pierce saw the change and wondered if God had somehow stirred her heart to understanding.

"And," Pierce added quickly, hoping that his words would reach her, "the blood which Christ shed for us is like that of the lambs' blood sprinkled over the doorposts of the Israelites, although more precious because it was the sacrifice of God's son rather than that of a simple beast. But both represent the shedding of blood in exchange for death passing us by. Christ died that we might not have to."

Darlene looked at him for a moment, and in those few precious seconds, Pierce believed that God had finally made Himself known to her. Perhaps there would be no instantaneous revelation. Perhaps it would be years before she would understand what had happened. However long it took, Pierce knew that seeds had been planted and he was confident that God could harvest Darlene's heart for His own.

ten

But God commendeth his love toward us, in that, while
we were yet sinners, Christ died for us. Romans 5:8

After sharing Passover with the Blackwells, Darlene knew
that she'd never be the same. It was impossible to stop
thinking about the words Dennison and Pierce had shared.
Also, it was impossible to not remember the joy in Father's
face and the certainty in which he shared his heart on the
matters of Christianity and Judaism. And, alas, it was also
impossible to forget Pierce Blackwell. His gentle smiles
pervaded her thoughts. His searching eyes and questioning
expressions made her realize that he wanted to know more
about her. But why? Why was Pierce paying her so much
attention? In the months that had passed since that *seder*
dinner, he had come by for visits, brought candy and trin-
kets (always for both herself and her father), and he seemed
completely determined to better know her mind on certain
issues.

What did she think of westward expansion? What did
she know about the new railroads? What had she read
about the western territories and states? Did she like to
travel? Would she ever consider leaving New York City?

Oy vey! But the man was annoying!

That night had not only given her reason to consider her
heart and soul, it had also changed forever her relationship
with her father. Abraham now openly attended church
with the Blackwells and more frequently was absent from
the synagogue. This made Darlene depressed and discour-
aged, but even more so, she found herself consumed by a
deep, unfillable void. Why did Tateh have to embrace

Christianity and turn away from the Hebrew faith? He hadn't announced the rejection of Judaism, so Darlene tried to keep hoping that her father was merely studying the *goy's* faith with a scholarly interest. But deep down inside, she knew it wasn't true.

In his bedroom, Darlene could hear her father at prayer. He would wear his *tallis,* the fringed prayer shawl of black and white. He would also have his *tefilin,* leather boxes, strapped to his forehead and left arm. Inside these boxes were the Scriptures of Exodus thirteen, verses one through ten, dealing with the remembrance of God bringing the Hebrew children out of bondage and commanding them to keep God's laws. On his head would be his *yarmulke* and from his mouth would come the familiar prayers she'd heard all of her life. These were the markings of his Jewish faith. Why then would he lay them aside in a few moments, eat breakfast with her, and go to the *goy's* church with the Blackwells?

Tears came to her eyes and she wiped at them angrily with the back of her sleeve. It wasn't right that her father should leave her so confused and alone. Why must she struggle through this thing? Why should there be such despair in her heart?

She brought bread and porridge to the table and set it down beside a huge bowl of fruit. She loved the summer months when fruits and vegetables could be had fresh. Fetching a pitcher of cream, Darlene tried to rally her heart to gladness. They had plenty and were well and safe. Her father's health had even revived a bit with the warmth of summer. Surely God was good and His protection was upon them, in spite of her father's search to better understand Christianity.

"Good morning, *Neshomeleh,*" Abraham said, coming into the kitchen. He reached a hand to his lips and touched the *mezuzah* as he always had.

Darlene smiled and came to greet her father with a hug. "Good morning, Tateh. Did you sleep well?"

"Yes, very well." His smile warmed her heart, just as his kiss upon her forehead put her at ease. "And you?"

"It is well with me, also."

They ate in companionable silence, but when Abraham had finished, he eyed Darlene quite seriously and said, "I have a favor to ask of you."

Darlene put down the dish she was clearing and asked, "What is it?"

"Sit."

She did as she was asked, but in her mind whirled a thousand possibilities. What was it that he would ask of her that required she sit down? "What do you want of me, Tateh?"

"Come with me today. Come to the Blackwell's church and be at my side. It is important to me and I only ask because it would mean a great deal."

"But why now? Why is it suddenly so important to you?" Darlene felt fear constrict her chest. It was difficult to breathe.

Abraham smiled lovingly and put his hand upon her arm. "Because today, I will accept Jesus into my heart."

"What!" She jumped up from the table. "You can't be serious!"

"Darlene, I have never been more serious. These long months I have searched for answers to questions that have eluded me all of my life. The knowledge given to me through the *Tanakh* and the New Testament has answered those questions."

"New Testament?"

Abraham smiled tolerantly. "It's the story of Jesus and His followers. It tells how believers in Christ should act and live. It filled my longing and took away my emptiness."

Darlene thought of her own longing and the emptiness that haunted her. She swallowed hard and sat back down in a rather defeated manner. "Then you are no longer of the faith. What of your friends and the shop? You will become as dead to them."

"Most likely," Abraham agreed. "But then, they haven't exactly been very friendly these last months anyway. I make a good living from people who are not Jewish, so the shop should not suffer overmuch."

"But Hayyim will leave us. How will you manage to work without help?"

"I'll advertise for a Christian. There must be plenty of Christian young men who would take up the job of tailoring."

Finally Darlene had to ask the one remaining question. "What of me? What of us? The cantor says I should leave you and live with Esther. He says you are a traitor and that should you reject your faith, I must leave or face the possibility of becoming a traitor as well."

Abraham shook his head. "There is nothing between us that must cause us to part. Come with me today and I believe you will come to understand my choice. In time, you may well come to make that choice for yourself and when you do, I want to be at your side."

Darlene stared at the table rather than meet her father's joyous expression. How could she be so sad when he was obviously so happy? How could she, who had listened to the words and advice of her father for all of her life, now reject his words because they seemed rash and contradictory to everything he had taught her?

"Please come with me today."

His pleading was more than she could bear. In that moment Darlene knew that should she be forever branded a traitor, she would still go with her father wherever he asked her to go. "I'll come with you," she whispered in a voice that barely contained her grief.

Abraham leaned over and kissed her on the head. "Thank you, my little soul. You are all that is left to me on this earth."

❧

Darlene was still thinking about his words when the Blackwell's carriage arrived and Dennison Blackwell stepped down to greet them. Darlene had put on her best gown, a pale blue muslin with huge gigot sleeves and lace trimming around the neck. It was a simple dress, yet it was her finest. In her mind she had imagined Pierce taking her by the arm to lead her into his church, and it was then that she wanted to look her very best.

"Good morning, Abraham, Darlene," Dennison said in greeting. "Have you ever known a more perfect day?"

"It is very lovely," Abraham said, then took hold of Darlene's arm. "My daughter will come with us today. Is there room in your carriage?" He looked up at the open landau where Eugenia and Constance Blackwell sat on one side, while Pierce occupied the other.

Dennison was at first quite surprised, but quickly enough a broad smile crossed his face. "There is plenty of room and you are very welcome to come with us, my dear."

Darlene felt her heart give a lurch when Pierce stood up and held out a hand to assist her up. "We're very glad to have you join us," he announced, while Eugenia gave her a harsh look of disdain. "You may sit here with Constance and my Aunt Eugenia."

Darlene put her gloved hand in his and allowed him to help her into the carriage. Eugenia looked away, while Constance smiled most congenially and made room for Darlene to sit in the middle. Abraham took his place between Pierce and Dennison and without further fanfare, they were on their way.

Immediately, Darlene was painfully aware of the contrast

to her best gown and the Blackwell women's Sunday best. Constance wore a beautiful gown of pink watered silk. The trimmings alone were worth more than Darlene's entire dress. Tiny seed pearls decorated the neckline and heavy flounces of lace trimmed the sleeves and skirt. Her hair had been delicately arranged in a pile of curls and atop this was a smart looking little hat complete with feathers and ribbons. A dainty pink parasol was over one shoulder to shade her from the sun and around her throat lay a strand of pearls, all perfectly white and equally sized.

Eugenia, of course, was attired even more regally in mauve colored satin. Darlene tried not to feel out of place, but it was obvious to anyone who looked at her that she felt completely beneath the standing of her companions.

Dennison introduced her to his sister and daughter, but only Constance had anything to say. "It's so nice to have you with us."

"Indeed it is," Pierce said with great enthusiasm.

❧

The church service was unlike anything Darlene had ever known. The women and men sat together for one thing, and somehow Pierce had managed to have her seated between himself and Constance. She was very aware of his presence. The smell of his cologne wafted through her head like a delicate reminder of her dreams. She couldn't suppress the fantasies that came to her mind and while they joined in to sing and share a hymnal, Darlene wondered what it might be like to marry Pierce and do this every Sunday.

What am I thinking? She admonished herself for such thoughts, while in the next moment her heart betrayed her again. To be the wife of Pierce Blackwell would mean every manner of comfort and luxury. It would mean having gowns of silk and satin. It would mean never having to worry about whether enough suits were made to pay the rent and grocer. She stole a side glance at Pierce. He caught her eye and winked, continuing the hymn in his deep baritone voice. Marriage to such a man would also mean love. Of this she had no doubt. Pierce Blackwell would make a most attentive husband.

The minister began his sermon by praying a blessing upon the congregation. Darlene watched for a moment, then bowed her head and listened to his words.

"Heavenly Father, we ask your blessing upon this congregation. We seek Your will. We seek to know You better. We ask that You would open our hearts to the truth, that we might serve You more completely. Amen."

Well, Darlene thought, *that wasn't so bad.* She relaxed a bit. Maybe this wasn't going to be such an ordeal, after all.

The minister, a short, older man, seemed not that different from the cantor. He wore a simple black suit and while he had no beard, his muttonchop sideburns were full and gave the appearance of at least a partial beard.

"It is good to come into the house of the Lord," he began. His words were of love and of a deep joy he found in God. Darlene couldn't help but be drawn to his happiness.

"God's love is evident to us in many ways," the minister continued. "God watches us with the guarded jealousy of a Father to His child. You fathers in the congregation would not allow a thief to sneak into your homes and steal your children from under your watchful eye, and neither does God allow Satan to sneak in and steal their hearts and souls.

"Just as you provide for your children, so God provides for us, His children. If your child was lost, you would seek him. If he was cold, you would warm him. If your son or daughter was hungry, you would give your last crumb of bread to feed them. So it is with God. He longs to give us good things and to care for us in His abundance." Darlene was mesmerized.

"God wills that none should be lost. He gave us His Son

Jesus Christ as a gift of love. Seeing that we were hopelessly lost, separated by a huge cavern of sin and despair, God sent his Son Jesus, to reconcile us to the Father. Is there anyone here who would not try to rescue your child from a burning house? Would any of you stand idly by and watch your children drown? Of course not. And neither would God stand by and watch us sink into the hopeless mire of sin and death, without offering us rescue.

"But what if you reached out a rope to your drowning child and they refused to take it? What if you tore open a passage in the burning house, but your child refused to come forward? So it is with God, who extends to us salvation through Jesus Christ, only to have us refuse to accept His gift." Darlene felt as though the minister was speaking to her alone. She'd never heard such words before. No wonder her father found himself confused. No wonder he questioned his faith.

"Will you be such a child?" the minister asked. "When God has offered you a perfectly good way back to Him, will you reject it? Will you throw off the lifeline God has given you in His Son? Will you die without knowing Christ as your Savior?"

Darlene could hardly bear the now serious expression on the minister's face. He seemed to look right at her and, inside her gloves, Darlene could feel perspiration form on her hands. She wanted to get up from her seat and flee from the building, but she couldn't move. Should the building have caught fire and burned down around her, Darlene knew that it would have been impossible to leave.

The minister spoke a short time more, then directed those who would receive Christ to step forward and publicly declare their repentance. Her mouth dropped when Abraham stood. She had known he would do this, but somehow watching it all happen, she didn't know what to think. A kind of despair and trepidation washed over her.

It was as if in that moment she knew a wall had been put in place to forever separate her from her beloved Tateh. A wall that she could only remove if she accepted Christ for herself.

As if sensing her fears, Pierce put her hand over hers and gave it a squeeze. This gesture touched Darlene in a way she couldn't explain. It was as if he knew her heart, and that somehow made it better. *Does he understand my loss?* she wondered.

Hearing a confession of faith from the man who had nurtured her so protectively, Darlene felt all at once as though he'd become a stranger to her. And yet, was it this that disturbed her most? Or was it the words of the minister? Words that made more sense than she would have liked to admit?

≥

The ride back home was spent in animated conversation between Dennison and Abraham, and Pierce and Constance. Eugenia remained stubbornly silent, while Darlene felt her mind travel in a million directions. All of which brought her continuously back to the dazzling smile and penetrating brown eyes of Pierce Blackwell.

"I'm glad you took time from the shop to accompany us today," Pierce told her.

"Do you work in your father's shop?" Constance asked in complete surprise.

Darlene nodded. "Yes. I do sewing for him."

"How marvelous. Tell me all about it," Constance insisted.

Eugenia harrumphed in obvious disgust and with that simple gesture, Darlene saw all her girlish dreams of marriage to Pierce fade. Of course, there had never been any real possibility of a lowly Jewess marrying a rich Christian socialite, but she had felt at least comforted by the possibility.

"My father is a tailor, as you know. We make suits and shirts, just about anything a man could possibly need for dressing."

"And they do it very well," Pierce added. "I have never owned such fine clothes."

"And you work with your father? Did you help with my brother's suit?" Constance asked, completely fascinated by this.

Darlene eyed the rich green frock coat and nodded. Pierce's gaze met hers and his lips curled automatically into a smile. "I didn't know that," he said, running his hand down the sleeve of his coat. "It only makes it all the more special."

Darlene felt her face grow hot. It made it special to her as well. She could remember running her hand down the fabric and wondering what Pierce would look like when it was completed. She had sewed the buttons onto the front with a strange sort of reverence, imagining as she worked how Pierce's fingers might touch them later.

"How wonderful to do something so unique!" Constance declared.

"It is hardly unique to do a servant's labor," Eugenia finally said. With these words came a silence in the carriage and a sinking in Darlene's heart.

Dennison frowned and Eugenia, seeming to sense that her opinion would meet with his disapproval, fell silent again. The damage was done, however. Darlene grew sullen and quiet, while Pierce looked away as if disgusted by the reminder of her station in life. There would never be a bridge between their worlds and the sooner Darlene accepted that, the happier she would be. But even forcing thoughts of Pierce from her mind did nothing to dispel the stirring memory of the minister's words that morning. Nor would it displace the image of her father going forward into acceptance of Jesus as Messiah. There was no going back now. There would be no chance of changing her father's mind about Christianity. But what worried Darlene more was that she wasn't sure she still wanted to change his mind.

eleven

*But the wisdom that is from above is first pure,
then peaceable, gentle, and easy to be intreated,
full of mercy and good fruits, without partiality,
and without hypocrisy.* James 3:17

❧

Pierce listened with bored indifference to Amanda Ralston's description of the new art museum her father had arranged to be built. The truth of the matter was, he was bored with the entire party. Amanda's party. Amanda and all her shallow, haughty friends.

The only reason he'd even come was that Eugenia had insisted on the matter until there was simply no peace in the house and even his father had asked him to do it as a favor to him. So it was because of this, Pierce found himself the center of Amanda's possessive attention.

"Darling, you haven't had any champagne," Amanda said with a coy batting of her eyes.

"I don't drink champagne and you know that full well." He tried not to frown at her. No sense having anyone believe them to be fighting.

Amanda pouted. "But then how shall we toast our evening?"

Pierce looked at her and shrugged. "I have nothing to toast, my dear. Why don't you go find someone who does?"

Amanda refused to be dealt with so harshly. "I had this gown made especially with you in mind. Don't you think it's lovely?" She held up her glass and whirled in a circle. The heavy gold brocade rippled in movement.

"It looks very warm," he said noncommittally. "I'm certain it will ward off the autumn chill."

Amanda was clearly losing patience with him. "Pierce, this gown cost over sixty dollars. The least you could do is lie about it, even if you don't like it."

"I see no reason to lie about it, and the gown is quite perfect for you. Sixty dollars seems a bit much. I know a great tailor, if your seamstress insists on robbing you."

"Oh, bother with you," she said, stomping her foot. "You are simply no fun at all."

"I didn't come here to have fun. I came because you and my aunt decided it should be so. There would have been no rest in my house if I'd refused."

"But Pierce," she said in a low seductive whisper, "didn't you want to see me? Don't you enjoy keeping company with me?"

Pierce looked at her in hard indifference. "I'd rather be mucking out stables."

"That's hideous!" She raised her arm as if to slap him, then thought better of it and stormed off. Pierce saw her exchange her half-empty glass for a full one before moving out of the room.

The rest of the evening passed in bits of conversation with one group and then another. Pierce, finally relieved of Amanda's annoying presence, found a moment in which to discuss westward expansion with several other men.

"It seems to me that we must settle this nation of ours or lose it," a broad-shouldered man with red hair was saying. "There's plenty who would take it from us. I say we move off the Indians and pay people to settle out west. Give them the land for free, although not too much land. Just enough to spark an interest."

"How would you move them all there?" asked an elderly gentleman. "There's not a decent road in this country. Even the civilized towns suffer for want of better roadways."

"True enough," said Pierce. "Perhaps the government could develop it. There's surely enough money in the U.S.

coffers to plow a few roads."

The redheaded man nodded. "Even so, it would take months, years, to make decent roads. We need people in the West now!"

His enthusiasm gave fuel to the spark already within Pierce's heart. "I've allowed myself some investments in Chicago. I've given strong thought to the possibilities of life there." This caused his companions to stare open-mouthed at him.

"You don't mean to include yourself in such a thing?" the older man questioned.

"Why certainly, I do." Pierce couldn't figure out why they should so adamantly declare the need for people in the West, yet find it unreasonable that he would consider such a thing.

"No, no. That would never do. You would have to deal with all manner of corruption and lowlife."

Pierce eyed the old man with a raised brow. "And I don't have to here? New York City is worse than ten western cities put together. Greed runs so rampant in this town that a man would sell his own soul if it promised a high enough return."

The redheaded man laughed at this. "Well, buying your soul out of hock seems a great deal easier than uprooting yourself and leaving the comforts of home behind. Monetary investments are one thing. Flesh and blood is quite another."

Pierce smiled. "I couldn't agree with you more. It is exactly for those reasons that I consider the possibilities of such a move."

It was then that Amanda chose to reappear. "What move are you talking about, darling?" She placed her hand possessively on Pierce's arm.

"It seems your friend would like to move out amongst the savages." The older man chuckled while the redheaded man continued. "I can just picture you at his side, Amanda dear. Dirt floors dusting the hems of your expensive gowns, six children grabbing at your skirts."

Amanda's laughter filled the air. "Oh, certainly Mr. Blackwell is making sport of the subject. He has too much here in the city to ever go too far. Isn't that true, darling?"

Pierce shook his head. "No, actually I'm quite seriously considering the move. Perhaps when spring comes and the weather allows for long-distance travel, I will resettle myself in Chicago."

"You can't be serious, Pierce." Her facade of genteel refinement vanished.

"I've only been telling you of my interest for months now."

Amanda waited until the other gentlemen had considerately moved away. She pulled Pierce along with her to a balcony off the main room and turned, prepared for a fight.

"Pierce, this is ridiculous. Your aunt assures me that it is your father's wish you marry and produce heirs. Now, while I have no desire to find myself in such a confining predicament, I would see fit to participate at least once in such a matter."

Pierce laughed. "Are you talking about giving life to a child, or suffering through a party for fewer than sixteen people?"

"This is a matter of grave importance; I won't stand your insults."

"Indeed it is a matter of grave importance." Pierce almost felt sorry for the young woman. She was clearly in a rage of her own creation. Her face was flushed and her eyes blazed with a fire all their own. She would have been pretty had she not been so conniving and self-centered. "Please hear me, Amanda. I have no desire to marry you. Not now. Not ever. I am not in love with you, which is the most important thing I believe a marriage should have. Without a mutual love and respect for each other, marriage would be nothing more than a sham of convenience. That kind of thing is not for me."

Amanda seemed to calm a bit. "Marriage is more than emotional entanglements, Pierce, and you know it as well as you know your bank account. To marry my fortune to yours would ensure our future. It would set forever our place in society. Imagine the possibilities, Pierce."

"I have, and they do not appeal to me."

"You aren't that stupid," she said, the caustic tone returning. "You are too smart to throw away your future. You've worked hard to set it into place."

"You are exactly right," Pierce replied.

She smiled with a seductiveness that ordinarily would have been charming. "I knew you'd see it my way."

"Oh, but I don't. I merely said you were right about my being too smart to throw away your future. I'm not about to sit around in houses that look fit only to be mausoleums, stuck in the middle of a city that's driven by greed and avarice and married to a woman who concerns herself only with parties and the value of her possessions." He turned to leave, but Amanda reached out to hold him.

"If you leave, I'll see you ruined!"

"Do what you will, Amanda, but do it without me."

He strode from the room without so much as a backward glance. He heard the sounds of the party behind him, the tinkling of glass, the faint strains of the stringed quartet, the laughter of shallow-minded associations. It was all a facade. There was absolutely nothing real or of value here for him.

He hailed a hack and gave the driver his address. Chicago loomed in his mind like an unattainable prize. Somehow, he would make his way west. Somehow, he would leave New York behind.

Darlene. The name came unbidden to his mind. Could he

leave her as well? Could he walk away from a woman he was now certain he loved? He couldn't suggest marriage, not with their religious differences. He couldn't take her away from her father, and even if he suggested Abraham accompany them west, Pierce didn't know if the old man was well enough to do so.

Chicago would mean leaving Darlene. Chicago would mean throwing off every matter of security ever known to him and going into the unknown alone. Could he do it? Could he leave the comforts of life as he knew it, and forge into the wilds of Illinois?

The hack pulled up to the red brick house and stopped. After paying the driver, Pierce made his way inside and found the house quiet. Grateful for this blessing, he made his way to the library. Tossing his frock and waist coat aside, Pierce undid his cravat and eased into a plush leather chair. On the small table beside him, a copy of the newspaper caught his eye.

Picking it up, he scanned the pages for anything of interest. "Irish Riots on the Wabash and Erie Canal," titled one article. Another announced the cause of some shipping disaster. He looked for something related to Chicago or travel west and found only one tiny article related to the suggested building of a railroad from New York State to the rapidly growing towns of Cincinnati and Chicago. It was such a small article and told with such a negative slant that Pierce was certain no one would paid it much mind.

He folded the paper, tossed it aside, and stretched out his long legs. *Dear God,* he began to pray, *what is it that I should do? I have no peace here. No happiness within my soul. I am as out of place as a fish taken from water. Society bids me be greedy when I would be generous, and tells me to have nothing to do with those who are beneath my status, when I would take all mankind to my heart.* He sighed. *Oh, God, please show me the way. Give me peace about the direction I should take. Give me a clear path to follow. Amen.*

"Whatever are you doing in here?" Eugenia questioned from the door. "I heard a carriage and couldn't imagine what you were doing home so early."

"I left because the party was not to my liking," he answered simply.

Eugenia frowned. "But what of Amanda? Surely she compensated you where the party was lacking."

"She was the one lacking the most," Pierce replied.

Eugenia looked behind her before entering the room and closing the door. "Pierce, you and I need to talk."

"We've talked aplenty as far as I'm concerned. Just leave it be." Exhaustion registered in his voice.

"I don't wish to cause you further grief, but you must understand," Eugenia began, "it is very important to your father that you settle down and marry. Amanda Ralston is everything you could ever hope to find in a wife. She'll be congenial. She'll run your home efficiently and she'll never interfere in your business. She's been groomed for just such a job since she was old enough to walk. Amanda knows her place and she'll benefit you in many ways."

"But I don't love her. I could never love her."

Eugenia grimaced. "Who could you love? That little Jew?"

Pierce narrowed his eyes. "Don't think to bring Darlene into this matter."

"Why shouldn't I? She clearly is a part of this matter. You fancy yourself in love with her, and I say forget it. She is not of your kind."

"And which kind would that be? The greedy kind? The selfish kind? Oh, wait, I know, maybe it's the kind who look down on others because they are different." Pierce got to his feet. "I'm glad she's not of those kind. But what you tend to forget because you're so mired in it yourself, is that I'm not of that kind either!"

"You are better than she is!" Eugenia said, blocking his escape by throwing herself between him and the door.

"No," he said, shaking his head. "I'm not. I'm not better than Darlene. I'm different in some ways, I'll give you that much. But I am not better. The Bible says that we should love one another, even as God loves us. Do you suppose God loves Darlene less because she's of Hebrew lineage? Jesus, Himself, is of such lineage! What if God loved me less because I'm not?"

"You cannot marry a Jew. Even by your own standards and beliefs you cannot do such a thing. You'd forever link yourself to a woman who would never believe as you do. Think of the irreparable harm you could do yourself."

Pierce picked up his coats and with little trouble, maneuvered Eugenia out of his way. "I'm finished discussing this. If you ever bring up the subject again, I will leave this house for good."

"I'm only trying to be wise about this, Pierce."

He realized that she truly believed this. Turning, he said, "Man's wisdom and God's are often two very different things. I've tried it man's way. Now I seek God's."

twelve

The preparations of the heart in man, and the answer of the tongue, is from the Lord. Proverbs 16:1

"So who are the flowers from?" Abraham asked his daughter.

Darlene stood holding a newly arrived bouquet of roses and the blush on her cheeks felt as warm a red as the flowers. "They're from Pierce Blackwell. He's coming this afternoon to. . .well. . .see me."

Abraham smiled and nodded. "That's good. I think he likes you."

"For whatever good that could ever do him," Darlene muttered and took the flowers upstairs to put on the kitchen table. Then, without thinking consciously of what she was doing, she hurried into her bedroom and changed her clothes.

Wearing a simple gown of green cotton and ivory ruching, Darlene tried to steady her nerves as she sewed a silk lining into a frock coat. Pierce had sent her flowers before, but never roses and never such a large bouquet. She felt a surge of anxiety and drew a deep breath. *I mustn't let him see me so jittery,* she thought. *I don't want him to think I'm drawing unmerited conclusions in this matter.* But she was. She was already imagining all of the most wonderful things that Pierce could come and tell her. Furthermore, she imagined how she might respond to just such things.

Even though Darlene knew and anticipated Pierce's arrival, it was still a surprise when he bounded through the door. He was dressed in a stylish brown suit which her father had made. His waistcoat of amber and orange might have appeared too loud on another man, but it seemed just right on Pierce.

"Hello," he said with a dashing smile and deep bow. "You look very pretty today."

Darlene put aside her sewing. "Thank you." She didn't know what else to say, so she folded her hands and said nothing more.

"You received my note, I presume."

"Oh, yes." She nodded, then remembered the roses. "The flowers are simply beautiful. I've put them upstairs. I was afraid down here someone might knock them over." She was also afraid that if Esther saw them she'd immediately begin questioning Darlene for all the facts.

"I thought you might enjoy them. I was passing a shop and saw them in the window. With winter coming on, I thought they might perk up the place a bit."

"They brighten the kitchen considerably."

The silence seemed heavy between them and Pierce searched for another topic. "And your father, is he well?"

"Yes. Well, he has a cold, but I'm hoping it won't be anything serious."

"Good."

"What of your family?" Darlene asked, raising her eyes to look upward.

"They are well. Constance had a birthday last week. She's sixteen now and feels very grown up."

"I remember sixteen quite well," Darlene replied. "I didn't feel very grown up at all. Of course we'd not been long in this country. I was struggling to improve my English and to make a good home for Tateh."

"I wish I could have known you then," Pierce said in a soft, almost inaudible tone.

Just then Abraham returned from an errand. His arms were full of brown paper-wrapped packages, and Pierce and Darlene hurried forward to take the burden from him.

"Tateh, you shouldn't have carried all of this yourself. I could have gone back and brought it home."

"Nonsense." He waved away her concern. "I'm an old man, but I'm still good for some things, no? Ah, Pierce, good day to you. I heard you were coming this afternoon."

"Yes," Pierce replied, putting the packages where Darlene motioned. "I would like very much to take Darlene for a walk. Would that be acceptable to you?"

Abraham smiled and struggled out of his coat. "It would be very acceptable. She works too hard now that Hayyim is gone."

"And you haven't found another assistant to help with the work, I take it?"

"No, but God will provide. He always has." Abraham's words would normally have comforted Darlene, but since all of the changes in her father's life, she was never certain whether she should take hope in such things.

"Of course He will. If I learn of anyone who might be adequate help, I'll advise them to come to you." Pierce then turned to Darlene. "Would you mind walking with me? It's a bit chilly, but otherwise very nice."

"I'll get my shawl," she replied. Now curiosity was taking over her fears. She had never known Pierce not to discuss every single matter of interest in front of her father. What was it that he wanted to say to her in private? And, if it wasn't a matter of discussing something with her, then why was he suggesting the walk? For a fleeting moment she hesitated. What if Esther saw her? *Oy!* What mutterings and innuendos she'd have to answer to then!

She pulled a cream-colored shawl around her shoulders. She'd only finished knitting it two days earlier, and this was her first real opportunity to show it off. Pulling a bonnet over her dark brown hair, Darlene hurried to join Pierce. If Esther saw her, she'd just deal with it later.

"I'm ready," she announced. "Tateh, are you sure you

can spare me?"

"Be gone with you already," Abraham said with a chuckle. "You can do Pierce more good than me."

And then they were outside and walking amicably down the street. When Pierce offered his arm, she hesitantly took it. Outside in the public eye it would mean dealing with more than just Esther. What would any of her friends say if they saw her walking with the *goy?* She squared her shoulders. It didn't matter. They'd all turned their backs on her father and she wasn't going to concern herself with what they thought. Oh, they were nice enough to her face and Esther still invited her over from time to time, but she knew they were all talking about her behind her back. And, she figured the only real reason Esther still called on her was for the simple purpose of gathering information.

"You don't seem to be listening to me."

Darlene looked up with an apologetic smile. "I do tend to get caught up in my thoughts."

"Yes, I know. That's why I suggested walking with you. I'll keep an eye for the freight wagons while you daydream. But, it comes with a price."

"Oh?"

"Yes," he nodded and added, "you must tell me what those dreams are about."

She shook her head. "They weren't really daydreams. I was actually thinking of the old neighborhood and how much it has changed."

"Has the neighborhood changed, or have you changed?"

"Some of both," she admitted. They walked past a fishmonger's cart and the heady scent of fish and other seafood assailed her nose. "Some things never change," she said, wrinkling her nose.

Pierce laughed and pulled her a little closer. "But change can be good, don't you think?"

"Is that why you've come to talk to me today?" *There,*

*she thought. I've just come right out with it and I don't
have to wonder any more what he's up to.*

Pierce wasn't phased by her boldness. "Yes," he answered
simply.

"So what change is it that you wish to discuss?"

"I'm leaving New York."

The words hit her like boulders. "Leaving? Where are you
going?" She tried hard to sound distant and unconcerned.

"Chicago. It's a fairly new town in Illinois. It's quite far
to the west and there's great opportunity to be found there."

"I see." She focused on the ground.

"Darlene, I wondered if you and your father might consider moving there also. I mean, I know what your father
has experienced here in the neighborhood. He's told my
father about some of the ugly letters. . ."

"What letters?" Darlene interrupted. "I've heard nothing
of letters."

Pierce looked genuinely embarrassed. "I'm sorry. I presumed that you knew."

"Tell me everything," she demanded, and halted in the
middle of the street as they crossed. "I have to know what
has been said."

"Surely you know already," he pulled at her arm, but
she held her place. "Come now, Darlene. I will share what
I know, but not in the middle of the roadway."

She allowed him to take her along and waited silently,
although impatiently, for him to tell her the truth.

"Apparently there have been some threats," Pierce said
as delicately as he could. "I believe the letters are harmless
enough, but they probably bear consideration. I know the
shop has been vandalized twice."

"But that was probably only street urchins," she said,
even now wondering about the truth of the matter.

"Your father thinks perhaps it is more than that." Pierce
pulled her into an alleyway and stopped. "You must know

that he doesn't wish to worry you, but, Darlene, I do fear for both of you. I know the ugliness of those who cannot accept what is different from what they know. Your Jewish friends can be just as prejudiced as my Christian friends."

She nodded, knowing that it was true. She could remember well the haughty stares of neighbors when her father stopped going to the synagogue. It was as if the Lewy family simply ceased to exist. Oh, they tried to be kind to her whenever she was alone, but ridicule followed even her. Especially when people asked her why she didn't leave Avrom and go to live with Esther.

"Chicago could be a new start for you both. I have property there and would be happy to set up a new shop for you. It could be as big as you like and I'm certain we could entice someone to sign on as an assistant to your father."

Darlene felt a single moment of excitement, then shook her head. "Tateh would never leave."

"Well, well. What have we here?"

"Looks like rich folk to me."

Pierce thrust Darlene behind him as he turned to face a group of filthy street rowdies. "What do you want?"

"Money, same as you uppity dandies," one of the taller boys said, coming a step closer.

"And jewels," another boy said. "Give us your lady's jewels."

There were five of them, with another two watching the street at the end of the alley. One of the boys produced a club and began whacking it in his hands. "Let's have it," he said in a low menacing tone.

Pierce moved a step back, pinning Darlene in place against the brick wall behind her. "I think we can work this out with no need of violence. Let the lady go and you may have my wallet."

"We'll have your wallet and the lady if we want," the boy replied.

Darlene peered around Pierce's shoulder. They couldn't be much more than teenagers, certainly not men. She was about to say something, but just then one of the five pointed at her.

"Wait a minute, Willy. That's the lady that helps us from the tailor shop. We can't rob her."

Pierce relaxed enough for Darlene to slip out from behind him. "I know your little brother. You must be Sam."

The boy nodded, looking rather sheepish. "Come on, guys. These are good folk."

The gang backed off and ran down the alley, signaling to their conspirators as they passed by. Pierce started to go after them, but Darlene reached out and took hold of him.

"Please let them go. They're only trying to survive. They wouldn't have hurt us."

"It didn't look that way to me," Pierce said angrily. "Scum and lowlife! That's all they're good for. The filth and despair of this neighborhood are all they know. Probably all they care to know. The lower classes always breed this kind of criminal element. Something should be done to clean up this neighborhood and rid it of the vermin."

"But Pierce," she said in a calm, soothing tone, "I am this neighborhood. My friends and family all live here. If you condemn them all because of the actions of a few, then you must surely condemn me as well."

This sobered him and he pulled her quickly back onto the main street before something else could happen. "I didn't mean it that way and you know it. I have only the highest admiration for you."

"But there are many in your circle of friends who believe we are nothing but Jewish scum. The Christ-killers. That's what they call us."

"But they can't blame you or your people for what a few. . ." he fell silent.

Darlene smiled, knowing that his words were about to

match hers. "People can be cruel without even knowing it. We came to this country for many reasons. One of the most inspiring was the growing hatred of Jews in my native home of Germany. That hatred started innocently enough with whispered insults and indifference. Gradually the name calling and assaults on our homes resulted in our being unable to live in certain areas and work at certain jobs. Can you imagine allowing such hatred to dictate the laws of the land?"

"How can you not hate them in return?" Pierce asked.

"I don't know. I suppose it is like Tateh says, 'To hate another requires that you keep the ugliness of their deed written on your heart so that you might hold it up to remember them by.'"

"Your father is very wise. Perhaps that is why his heart was so open to the Word of God regarding Jesus."

Darlene nodded. "It may well be." She felt the familiar stirrings and knew that, more than anything else, she would like for Pierce to better explain Jesus to her. "I wonder if you would tell me a bit about your Jesus."

If Pierce was surprised by her words, he didn't say so. "Jesus came as a baby to this world. You know of the Christmas celebration?" Darlene nodded. "We celebrate His birth and give gifts to each other in honor of the day. In truth, Jesus came to a lowly Jewish couple, a carpenter and his wife. Joseph and Mary. He was a gift from God to the world. He came among men, because God wanted to draw all men to Him. He wanted to give man a path to forgiveness and eternal life. Jesus said in John fourteen, 'I am the way, the truth, and the life: no man cometh unto the Father, but by me.' So you see, we believe that by accepting Jesus as Messiah and repenting of our sins, we accept the way to God and eternal life."

They were back to the shop by now, but Darlene wished they could walk on forever. She found her heart clinging to every single word Pierce said. Could it be true? Could Jesus really be the Messiah her people looked for? Had they simply missed the signs or had they willingly ignored them?

"And you believe all of this, without any doubt at all?" she asked softly, looking up to find Pierce's tender expression.

"Without any doubts or fears," he whispered, taking her small hands in his own.

"But what makes you so certain?" She felt a tingle of excitement shoot up her arm and goosebumps form on her skin.

"He makes me certain," Pierce replied. "He makes me certain deep within my soul."

thirteen

*And she shall bring forth a son, and thou shalt call
his name Jesus: for he shall save his people from
their sins.* Matthew 1:21

❧

They stood by the shop door for what seemed a long time
before Darlene finally turned the handle and went inside.
Pierce followed her, but paused just inside the door.

"Think about what I said," he told her.

Darlene couldn't help but think of all the things he'd
said. Things about leaving New York, wanting her and her
father to go to Chicago, and that Jesus loved her. "I will,"
she promised. And then without warning, he gave her one
more thing to think about.

Taking her face in his hands, he placed a very light kiss
upon her lips. "I love you," he whispered. Darlene opened
her eyes in a flash of confusion and wonder. She stared up at
him, not really believing she'd heard the words accurately.

As if reading her mind, he repeated them. "I love you. I
think I always have."

Before she could say a single word, he turned and left the
shop, gently closing the door between them. To Darlene
it was a moment she would always remember. Pierce
Blackwell loved her and had kissed her as a token of his
affections. Touching her hand to her lips, she could
scarcely breathe. *He loves me?* It wasn't mere infatuation
on her part? She thought of the hundreds of daydreams
she'd had about him. Dreams of marriage and love,
romance, and a future as Pierce Blackwell's wife.

"Darlene, is that you?" her father called from upstairs.

"Yes, Tateh." She could barely say the words. Her voice

117

seemed incapable of working properly and her legs felt like leaden weights.

"Are you all right? Is Pierce still with you?"

"No. I mean, yes I'm all right, but Pierce has gone home." At least, she presumed he'd gone home.

She forced her legs to work and pulled the bonnet from her head as she made her way upstairs. She thought about Pierce and his words about Jesus. *Tateh believes in Jesus,* she thought. *Pierce believes in Jesus. Why should I not believe in Him just because all of my life I've been taught one way?*

At the top of the stairs she paused. The only person in the entire world who could help her now was her father. "Tateh," she called, coming into the kitchen where he sat eating a bowl of soup, "I need to talk to you."

Abraham put down his spoon and motioned her to take a chair. "Is something wrong? You look as though you bear the weight of the world."

Darlene put aside her bonnet and shawl and sat down. "Tateh, there are things I want to know about."

"What things?"

She took a deep breath. "Pierce told me that Jesus came to make people a way back to God. He said Jesus said that He was the way and that no one could get to God except by going through Jesus."

"That is true."

"But our people do not believe in Jesus as Messiah. They don't believe that they need someone to make a way for them to God." She paused, reflecting on a lifetime of training. "They believe each man is responsible for his own sin, so therefore how could Jesus take on the responsibility for all mankind and settle the matter for even those people yet to come?"

Abraham smiled. "Because God loves us, He showed mercy. He gave Jesus as a means to demonstrate his love.

Not only for the people of His own time, but for the future generations. He was born purposefully to save His people, and Darlene, we are His people, even before the Gentiles."

"But our people rejected him as Messiah. They saw Him die and presumed that He couldn't possibly be what they expected."

"Not only that, but Jesus made a great many people, especially those who were high Jewish authorities, very uncomfortable. His way would bring change and people often resent change."

Darlene thought instantly of Pierce and his words about change being good. "But if Jesus was the Messiah we looked for, why have our people suffered so? Are we being punished for rejecting Him? Is God reckoning with us for something we didn't understand?"

"Who can know God's mind?" Abraham said with a shrug. "I suppose I look at the world and our place within the bounds of mankind and I say, 'There are many problems here.' Not only the Jews suffer. Think about history. Even the Christian church has had its bloody times. The world has seen plagues and sufferings throughout. Even here in America the plight of the slave is evidence of injustice. They were taken from their homes and forced away from families and loved ones in order to work for people they didn't know. Many people are hurting and suffering. I don't think God has forgotten us. Remember the sufferings of Job?"

"Yes, but how can God continue to let such things go on? Can't He see what is happening?"

Abraham shrugged. "I think He keeps better watch than you imagine. It's a matter of trusting, Darlene. We have to have faith just as the children of Israel had faith that God would lead them through the desert."

"Yes, but God allowed them to wander for forty years," she added.

"But was that because of God's indifference or their sin?"

Darlene nodded. "I guess I see what you're saying. We often suffer our lots in life because of our own disobedience. By our own hand we create the miseries of the world, is that right?"

"I believe so," Abraham replied.

"Then the Jewish rejection of Jesus could well have something to do with our people's miseries. Not because God is angry that we rejected the Messiah, but because we continue in blindness to seek another way."

"Perhaps."

Darlene looked at her father and in her heart she felt the birth of something very precious. It was a trust in God that she'd never before known. "Tateh, is Jesus the Messiah?"

Abraham smiled. "He is."

"And you are certain? There is no room for doubt in your heart?"

"None."

"That's what Pierce said."

"And what did you think of that?"

Darlene sat back and breathed a deep breath. What did she think of it? Wasn't that part of the reason she was seeking out her father's advice? "He seemed very confident. I suppose I envy that confidence. When I am with my friends, I feel there is an emptiness which no one can explain. When I was little, I thought like you, that it had to do with Mother's death. When I got older, my women friends told me that I was simply yearning for a husband and family. But Tateh, I don't believe that's what I'm looking for.

"There are many women in our community who are married with many children of their own, and yet, I know there is a void within them as well. I've talked to Rachel and Dvorah and even Esther and all of them have known this emptiness. Esther says she fills it with work and other things."

"Mostly gossip and sticking her nose where it doesn't belong, no?" Abraham said with a smile.

"It's true Esther is an old busybody, but perhaps she is one because she is empty and lonely inside. Who knows?" Darlene replied with a shrug.

"God knows and He sees all."

"I do believe that." She thought of Pierce's certainty and of her father's unwavering faith. "And you believe that the Messiah has already come and that He is Jesus. You believe that the Christians are right and that we Jews are wrong."

"I believe that Jesus came to save all people. I believe the faith of my fathers is valid and important, but falls short of a complete understanding of God's love and mercy. You must understand, Darlene, I do not throw away my Jewish heritage to take up one of Christianity. I am a Jew, but I also believe in Jesus."

Darlene shook her head. "I don't see how this can be so. I've been taught since I can first remember that you cannot be both Jewish and Christian. I've been taught that Jesus is not the Messiah we seek, for if Jesus was Messiah why did He not set up his Messianic Kingdom and restore Jerusalem? I so want to believe what you say is true, but a lifetime of beliefs stand between me and Jesus."

Abraham took hold of her hand and patted it lightly. "God will make a way through the desert. Just as He made a way for the Israelites so long ago. You mustn't be afraid to let God show you the way, however. Pray and trust Him, and let Him show you the truth."

"But how will I know that it is the truth, Tateh?" She searched his face, knowing that her expression must surely register the pleading of her soul.

"You will know," he said smiling. "You will know because God will give you peace of heart and mind."

In the warmth of his bed, Pierce awoke in the middle of the night with only one thought He had to pray for Darlene! He felt the call so urgently that it wouldn't let him be

"Dear God, what has happened? What is it that I should pray about?" He struggled with the covers of his bed and went to the fireplace to rekindle the flames.

The fire caught and grew, bringing with it a warm orange glow to the room. Sitting cross-legged in front of the hearth, Pierce reached up to the nightstand and took down his Bible. He read for several minutes, but again the urgency to pray was upon him. He buried his face in his hands, struggling against the image of Darlene's innocent expression after his kiss.

"Father," he began in earnest. "I love Darlene, but I know Your Word tells me not to be unequally yoked with unbelievers. I can't help loving her, though. She is a special part of my life and I've already told You that I will walk away and go to Chicago without her, if that's what You want me to do."

Utter misery took hold of him and it felt as though a part of his heart was being ripped in two. When had she become so important to him? When had he lost his heart so completely to her? There had to be a way to bridge the distance. There had to be an answer he was not seeing. *I love her, and I want her to be my wife!* But even as he acknowledged this truth, God's Spirit overshadowed it with the Word. What fellowship could light have with darkness?

"But God, she's not evil. She's faithful to serve You in her own way."

The words seemed to echo in his mind. "Her own way." Not God's way.

This did nothing to lay aside the need to pray and so Pierce tried to refocus his thoughts and pray just for the woman he loved. "Darlene needs to know You, Father. She needs to know that You love her and she needs to accept Jesus into her heart. Please dispel her fears and let her mind be open to the truth. Give her peace, dear God. Let her come unto You and know the joy and contentment of being reconciled."

Assurance flooded Pierce's soul. This was good and right and exactly what he needed to do. Until the wee hours of the morning, Pierce continued to pray for Darlene and her father. It was as if a spiritual battle was raging somewhere and Darlene's soul was the prize. Pierce was not about to let go of her, and he knew that God would not let go of her either. Feeling a stillness within, Pierce collapsed into bed just as the horizon brought the first signs of morning light.

"I love her, God," he whispered, "but I give her to You."

fourteen

For we know in part, and we prophesy in part.
But when that which is perfect is come,
then that which is in part shall be done away.
1 Corinthians 13:9, 10

❧

December came in with bitter cold and strong winter winds.
Darlene found it impossible to keep the house warm, and in
spite of her efforts, Abraham grew weaker. When he finally
succumbed to his illness and remained in bed, Darlene
knew that her worst fears were coming true. Somewhere,
deep down inside, she knew that her father was dying.

She tried to busy herself so as not to think about such
morbid things. She took what few orders she could get
for suits and cut them herself, relying on the briefest of
measurements lest she cross over the line of propriety by
measuring the men herself. She was up before the light of
day and still working long into the hours of the night.
Cutting patterns out of heavy wool, stitching through
thick layers until her fingers bled, and constantly worry-
ing about her father. And through it all, her heart reflected
on the words of her father and of Pierce. She thought of
God's love and the hope that was found in the belief that
Messiah would one day come and properly restore all
things. If only Messiah would come now.

Every week when Sabbath came, she would light the
candles and ask the blessing, but her heart sought something more. Her soul yearned to understand in fullness the
mystery that eluded her. Sometimes when her father slept,
she would creep in to sit by his side, and as she sat there she
would pray for understanding. Once, she even picked up his

124

Yiddish New Testament, a gift from Dennison Blackwell. Thumbing through the pages she found a most intriguing passage in a section marked, "The First Letter of Paul the Apostle to the Corinthians." Chapter thirteen was all about love. The writer said, in his own way, that even if he were really good and had the best of intentions and kept the faith, but didn't have love, it was all for nothing.

Verse twelve caught her attention and stayed with her throughout the days which followed. "For now we see through a glass, darkly; but then face to face: now I know in part; but then shall I know even as also I am known." That's how she felt. Like she was seeing God and the world through a dark, smudgy glass. There were parts that seemed glorious and too wondrous to speak of. Like Messiah and God's ability to forgive. There were also parts which seemed clouded and vaguely open to understanding. Like eternity and Messiah's coming and whether her people had been wrong to reject Jesus.

Sitting as close to the kitchen stove as possible, Darlene worked at her sewing and allowed her thoughts to drift to Pierce. She hadn't seen him in weeks and she couldn't help but wonder if he'd already left for Chicago. He'd said that he loved her, but apparently there was nothing more he could say or do, for he'd never written or come back to say more. Perhaps it was just as well. They lived in two very different worlds.

Darlene tried to imagine him at home. No doubt the comfort of his wealth kept him from too seriously considering his love for a Jewess. Still, he had asked her to come west with him. He'd promised to help her and Tateh. A shop in Chicago! She tried to envision it. Pierce had said it could be as large as she liked. How wonderful it would be to plan out such a thing. She would make all the rooms on the ground floor so that her father wouldn't have to trudge up and down the stairs. She'd put their rooms at the very back and make it so that the shop could be completely closed away from the living quarters. And they'd have huge fireplaces and stoves to keep the building warm.

A loud knock sounded on the downstairs door, causing Darlene to nearly drop her scissors. She put aside her sewing and hurried down the stairs. *What if it's Pierce?* she wondered and smoothed back her hair with one hand while adjusting her shawl with the other.

She peered through the window shade and was surprised to find Esther standing on the other side. "Esther, it's freezing outside; you shouldn't have come out!" she chided.

"It was colder in the old country. I can bear a little cold," she said, hurrying through the door nevertheless. She held out a covered pot. "It's soup for your father. I've heard it said he is ill."

Darlene took the pot. "Yes, he is. He's bedridden and I'm afraid it will be a long, slow recovery. The doctor says he's sick with consumption."

"Feh!" Esther spat out in disgust. "He is sick because he has angered God!"

"How can you say such things?" Darlene asked angrily. "Did my father not provide for you when you had nothing?"

"It is true enough, but he had not forsaken the faith of his ancestors then. Now he has and God is punishing him for his waywardness. Mark my words, Darlene, you will fall into corruption and be lost as well. Don't think I haven't heard that you keep company with the *goyim*. You will be forever lost if you turn from God."

"I'm certain that is true," Darlene replied. "But neither I nor my father have done that." She paused and some of the anger left her. "Esther, have you never wondered about Messiah?"

"What's to wonder? Messiah will come one day and that will be that. Of course, we should live so long!" The wind picked up and played at the edges of their skirts.

Darlene shivered and she knew that Esther must be cold. "Do you want to come upstairs and talk?"

"No," Esther replied. "Rachel and Dvorah are helping me to make a quilt for Mrs. Meyer."

"And you didn't ask me to help?" Darlene tried not to show how hurt she was. She would no doubt have begged off anyway.

"It is better you decide your loyalties first. There's been a great deal of talk about you and Avrom. You should set yourselves right with God and seek His forgiveness. Then we will talk again."

"But my heart is right with God," Darlene protested. "I've done nothing wrong."

"You are the daughter of your father. Avrom's house is in danger because his heart is corrupt with *goyishe* reasonings. You must convince him to repent and then perhaps God will heal him of his afflictions. Don't forget about the sins of the fathers being revisited upon the children."

"And just what are you saying by that?"

Esther's forehead, already wrinkled with age, furrowed as she raised her snowy white brows. "Only that you are close to corruption by staying here."

Darlene felt her temper dangerously close to exploding. Exhaustion was making her bold and unfearing. "Tateh has God's wisdom and a peace of soul that I have yet to find in our congregation. We say that Messiah will come and make all things right, and I'm telling you that Messiah may well have already come to try."

Esther put her hands to her ears. "I'll not listen to any more. You're a *meschuggene* just like your father! Better you should leave him now!"

"No, I won't desert him like everyone else. It was good of you to bring him soup. I will bring you back the pot later tonight."

Esther seemed to have nothing more to say and quickly

left the shop. Darlene took the soup upstairs, poured it into her own pot, then put it on the stove to keep warm. She went to check on her father and found him awake and seemingly better.

"Tateh, Esther has brought you some soup. Would you like some now?"

"No, just come and sit with me," he said in a weak voice. "I would tell you some things before it's too late."

"Shh, Tateh! Don't say such things."

Abraham tried to sit up, but he was too weak. Falling back against his pillow, he reached out a hand to Darlene. "Please hear me," he said, breaking into a fit of coughing.

She took his hand and sat down on the edge of his bed. He looked so very old and fragile now. Once her Tateh had been a pillar of strength and she looked to him for the courage she lacked. Now, she wished with all of her heart that something could be done to help him. But the doctor said there was nothing to be done. Nothing could help rid him of the consumption which seemed to ravage his lungs.

Darlene waited in silence, not moving so much as a muscle lest she cause him to cough even harder. He struggled for breath and finally the spell subsided. "I'm going to a better place," he said softly. "You must promise me that you will not be afraid."

Darlene knew better than to argue with him. "I promise," she said, wondering if she could really keep her word.

"And another promise," he whispered.

"What is it, Tateh?"

"Promise me that you will think about Jesus. I don't want to die knowing that you might forever be lost."

Tears came to her eyes as she hugged his hand to her face. "I can't bear for you to talk about death. I can't bear to think of life without you."

"Jesus is the true Messiah. I want very much for you to know that. Don't be afraid of the world and the things which would hide the truth from you." He began coughing anew and this time when the attack subsided, there was blood at the corners of his lips.

"I want to know that Jesus is truly the Messiah," she said. Tears fell upon his hand as she kissed it. "I don't want you to leave me."

"We'll never be parted again if you accept Jesus as your Atonement," he said in a voice filled with as much longing as Darlene felt in her heart.

"What must I do?"

Abraham's eyes seemed to spark with life for a brief moment. "You must only ask Him into your heart. Ask His forgiveness for your sins, and He will give it to you!"

Darlene thought of this for a moment. A peace filled her and she knew in an instant that it was the right thing to do. There was no image of Pierce or her dying father, or the ugliness of her friends and neighbors; there was only this growing sensation that this was the answer she had sought all along. Jesus would fill the void in her heart and take away her loneliness.

"Then let it be so," she whispered. "I want Jesus to be my Savior."

"Baruch Ha-Shem," Abraham gasped and closed his eyes. "Blessed be The Name."

Darlene saw the expression of satisfaction that crossed her father's face. It was as if a mighty struggle had ceased to exist. Was this all that had kept him alive? Was this so important that he couldn't rest until he knew Darlene believed in Jesus?

Outside the wind howled fiercely and Darlene remembered that she needed to return Esther's pot. "Tateh, I must go to Esther's and take back her soup pot. I won't be gone but a minute."

"Wait until tomorrow," he said in a barely audible whisper.

"I think it might well snow before then and I'd rather not have to go out in it. I'll only be a few minutes and besides, no one will bother me. Ever since that day when Pierce and I were accosted by the rowdies, I've had the assurance of Willy and Sam that we'd be safe. They even keep an eye on the building in case anyone wants to vandalize it. I think they're the reason our so-called friends haven't broken any more windows in the shop."

Abraham drew a ragged breath and opened his eyes. "Then God go with you."

She leaned down and kissed his cold, dry forehead. "And with you."

Pausing at the door, Darlene kissed her hand and touched the *mezuzah*. The action was performed as a reminder of how she should always love God's Word and keep it in her heart. In that moment, it became more than an empty habit. In that moment, Darlene was filled with a sense of longing to know all of God's Words for His people. She glanced back at her father and felt a warmth of love for him and the Messiah she had finally come to recognize.

"Jesus," she whispered the name and smiled.

fifteen

And the world passeth away, and the lust thereof:
but he that doeth the will of God abideth for ever.
1 John 2:17

❧

Pierce sat with his shirt sleeves rolled up and his collar unbuttoned—a sure sign that he was hard at private work. Within the confines of his room, he couldn't help but wonder if he'd miss New York when the time came to leave. When in Europe, home had been all that he could think of. But then thoughts of Eugenia's demanding ways, his father's constant absences, and Constance being torn between the two adults she loved most in the world would dissolve any real homesickness. Perhaps it would be the same when he moved west to Chicago.

He looked at the latest letter he'd received from Chicago. He'd hired a well-respected contractor and was already the proud owner of a hotel. Well, at least the frame and foundation were in place. The five-story building was, as the letter put it, enclosed enough to allow indoor work during the harsh winter months. There would, of course, be a great deal of interior work to be done. Pierce remembered the blue-prints with pride. The hotel would stand five stories high and have one hundred twenty rooms available for weary travelers. Located close to where packets of travelers were deposited off of Lake Michigan, Pierce knew his hotel would be the perfect moneymaker. And, with more than enough room to expand, Pierce had little doubt he could enlarge his establishment to house more than two and maybe even three hundred people.

Leaning back in his chair, Pierce tried to imagine the

finished product. Brick with brass fixtures would make a regal first impression. Especially to that tired soul who longed for nothing more than a decent bed and perhaps a bath. There were also plans for a hotel restaurant, and Pierce had felt a tremendous sense of satisfaction when he'd managed to secure one of the finest New York chefs for his hotel. It had cost him triple what it would have cost to hire a less experienced man, but Chef Louis de Maurier was considered a master of cuisine and Pierce knew his presence would only improve the hotel's reputation.

Of course, the fine imported oak and mahogany furniture he planned to ship would be a tremendous help as well. Each hotel room would be supplied with the very best. Oak beds with finely crafted mattresses. The best linens and fixtures money could buy would also draw the better paying customer. He thought of how there would be many people who couldn't afford such luxury and immediately thoughts of a lower-priced, less formal hotel began to formulate in his mind. He could build a quality hotel and supply it with articles which were sturdy and durable, but not quite as fine. Each room could have several beds and this way poorer folks could share expenses with several other people. He could charge by the bed, instead of by the room. *Chicago was going to be a real challenge,* he thought, and scratched out several of his ideas onto paper.

Then, as always happened during his daydreams, Pierce's mind conjured images of Darlene. He'd purposefully left her alone after suggesting she and her father come west. More importantly, he'd left her to consider that he loved her. He hadn't intended to tell her that, but there was a desperation in him that hoped such words just might turn the tide. If she knew how he felt, perhaps she would encourage her father to consider the trip to Chicago. And already, Pierce was prepared for just such a decision. He'd managed to locate a doctor whose desire it was to relocate to Chicago. For passage and meals, the man had agreed to travel with Pierce and act as private physician to Abraham Lewy. This way, Pierce was certain that Darlene could find no objections to the idea of going west.

He frowned as he thought of the stories he'd been told by his father. Stories of how Darlene's friends had turned away from the Lewy family. Stories of how Darlene was forced to sew what few orders she could obtain by herself. He tried not to think of her shoulders bent and weary from the tasks she bore. He tried, too, not to think of her face marred with worry over the health of her father, which Dennison had already told him had been considerably compromised by the cold winter weather.

I love her, Lord, he prayed. *I love her and want her to be my wife, but I won't go against You on this. If You would only turn her heart toward You and open her eyes to the need for salvation, I would happily take her as my wife and love her with all of my heart.*

"Pierce? Are you in there, Son?" Dennison Blackwell questioned.

"Yes, come in." Pierce yawned and straightened up.

Dennison opened the door. "I wondered if you would join me for coffee in the library. There are some things I think we should discuss."

"Things? Such as?"

"Such as Chicago and your insistence to cast away the world you know for the wilds of the West and what you do not know."

Dennison seemed so genuinely upset that Pierce instantly got to his feet. "I would be happy to put your mind at rest."

He followed his father down the hall and into the library which stood at the top of the main staircase. Dennison closed the door and motioned Pierce to take a seat, while he himself began to pace.

"I know you're a grown man and have every right to the future of your choosing, but I cannot say that this idea of yours doesn't bother me. Chicago is hundreds of miles away and travel is precarious at best." He held up his hand lest Pierce offer any objections. "Yes, I know the Erie Canal is making travel to the Great Lakes much easier. I've even managed to obtain information on a variety of wagon trains and stagelines that go west."

"You've left out the possibility of taking a sailing vessel to New Orleans and then going up the Mississippi and across Illinois," Pierce said with a grin. "Oh, Father, you really shouldn't be so worried. I know this is where God is directing me to go. There's so much to be done and men of my standing, with the capital to back them, can not only make a huge fortune, but benefit the masses who also are dreaming of a new start. Chicago has nearly four thousand residents and it is projected that by 1840 there will be twice that many people."

"That's all well and good, but. . ."

"Father, why don't you come west with me? We could build an empire! I still own a great deal of land in Chicago and we could develop it together."

Dennison smiled sadly at this. "I thought we were doing that here in New York."

"But I can't bear the snobbery of this town much longer. The prejudices are enough to drive me mad."

"And you think Chicago will be without its own form of prejudice?"

Pierce knew his father had a point. "I'm sure they do have prejudice, but they aren't formed around the tight little society that New York has made for itself. I've never known another town, with the exception of Boston, that holds its lofty council above all others and looks down its nose at those considered beneath it."

"Then you haven't looked very close," Dennison said with a smile. For some reason this seemed to put him at ease and he took a chair across from Pierce and poured a cup of steaming black coffee. "I've traveled to some of the same places you have. London. Paris. Munich. They all have their 'tight little societies' as you put it. You know as well as I do how laws have been passed in Germany to discriminate against the Jews. Some towns are even forbidden for them to live in, and others are denying them the right to own property and businesses. I'm telling you, Pierce, there is no place in this world that is without its own form of prejudice."

Pierce poured his own coffee and sighed. "I know you're right. It just seems a shame to watch people so divide themselves. Their greeds and lusts take over and they give little consideration for those who suffer."

"It was no different in Jesus' time. You must understand, Pierce, there will always be those who suffer injustices. All you can do is your very best to see that you aren't a part of it and that you render aid where you can."

"But don't you understand? That's what I'm trying to do now. In leaving New York, I leave behind their ways and their snobbery. I say to them, in essence, enough is enough and I will no longer be party to your corruption. And I am already prepared to render aid. I found a Jewish doctor who is a new Christian. He desires to go west and I have offered to pay his passage to Chicago in turn for his acting as private physician to Abraham Lewy."

"Abraham? He has agreed to go with you to Chicago?"

"No, but I'm certain that once I speak to him of the benefits he will want to go."

"And if he doesn't?"

Pierce shrugged and pushed back thick brown hair which had fallen onto his forehead. "I don't know. I guess I kind of figured if I made him an attractive offer, he'd naturally want to come along."

"And Darlene? Was she a part of the attractive offer?"

Pierce grinned. "Well, of course Darlene is included. I mentioned to her the idea and told her I'd help her father establish a new shop and home."

"And what did she say?" Dennison eyed his son quite seriously.

This question took some of the wind out of Pierce's sails. "She didn't think he'd want to go."

"I thought as much. You see, Abraham and I have often discussed the matter of moving west. Many of the Jews who came here over the last ten years have done so only with westward expansion in mind. They aren't comfortable in the large eastern cities where people are cruel with hate and prejudice. They are more inclined to migrate west and form their own towns and societies. Abraham considered such a thing, but he was sure that his age was against him. Thinking he was too old, he settled here and found friends he could trust."

"But I want very much for them to know peace and to be accepted into the community. Now that Abraham is a Christian, surely people will take him in and treat him respectfully."

"They will always be Jewish by blood. They look like Jews, they sound like Jews, they have Jewish names. People are going to know. Whether they worship in a synagogue or a church, people are going to think of them as Jews. And, you're forgetting one very important thing. Darlene is still of the Jewish faith."

"But it is my prayer that she'll come to know Christ."

"But until she does, Pierce, she is still very much separated from you in her beliefs. You have fallen in love with this woman, I know that. But I'm telling you that marriage to one such as her can only spell disaster for you both."

Pierce only frowned and sipped at the hot liquid in his

cup. He felt the familiar resentment of wanting something that he knew he couldn't have.

"If you were to marry her without her having accepted Christ, who would preform the ceremony? A rabbi? A minister? Then, too, would you attend a church or a synagogue and when would you actually honor the Sabbath? On Saturday or Sunday? What happens, even if you both amicably decide to worship God your own way, when children come along? Will you raise them as Christians or as Jews? Can't you see, Pierce, there is no peace in a divided house. You cannot walk both paths and remain true to either one. You are a Christian. Your foundation for living is in the salvation you know in Christ. You base your beliefs on the Christian Bible and you know that the teachings there are absolute truth. To marry Darlene would be to cast off all that you know as right."

"But Darlene is only one small issue. Even men in the Bible married women of other cultures and nations."

"That's true. But Ahab married Jezebel when she was still an idolatress and it was a disaster. Samson fell in love with Delilah and it led him into tragedy."

"But what of Ruth the Moabitess?"

"Yes, she accepted the Jewish faith and culture and so became acceptable for Boaz to marry. Do you see Darlene giving up her faith and culture for you?"

Pierce put down the cup and shook his head. "I wouldn't want her to do it for me. I want her to know Jesus for herself. I want her to be saved because God has opened her eyes to the truth."

Dennison nodded. "I'm glad to hear you say that, because if she changes faiths for you, and not because God has so moved her heart, it will never take root and grow in her heart."

"I know," Pierce replied, and indeed he did know it full well. Wasn't it the same thing that had given his heart hours of frustration and grief? Wasn't it the very burden he had laid at his Savior's feet, begging for hope and a satisfactory solution?

"Are you completely certain that God is leading you to Chicago?"

Dennison's question hit a spot deep in Pierce's heart. "Yes. I feel certain."

"How do you know for sure that it is right?"

Pierce sighed. "Because I have such peace about going. Even," he paused, "when I count what I must leave behind, I know that it is the right thing to do."

"And if those things left behind include Darlene Lewy?"

"I told God I'd leave her, too." Pierce looked up, his eyes filling strangely with tears. "Don't think it's easy for me to say these things. Don't think it's easy for me to leave you and Constance, either. But I know that I have to do it. I know this is right. I've prayed and considered the matter and always the answer is, 'Yes, go to Chicago.' I can't forsake what I know is God's will for my life."

"Nor would I ask you to," Dennison said, leaning forward to place his hand over his son's. "It won't be easy to let you go again, but if you are this convinced that God is leading you, then I must have peace in it and trust Him to know the way that is best. It won't be easy for me, either. It will be lonely here without you, and there will be a void that only you can fill. But, alas, children do grow up and find their own way. I'm gratified to know that you seek God's counsel. It makes me confident that I have done right by you."

"Of that you may be certain," Pierce replied, putting his hand in his father's. He squeezed it gently.

Outside, the wind died down a bit and as it did the sound of distant bells could be heard clanging out in the night. Fire was a common thing in New York and the fire departments were the best in the world. Each station had its own signals and this was clearly a signal for their own neighborhood.

Pierce jumped up and ran to the window, wondering if he could see where the fire might be. An eerie sensation ran through him and the hairs on the back of his neck stood up. Inky blackness shrouded the town and even the bit of moon overhead did nothing to light the darkness. His heart began to race faster with each clang of the bell.

"I can't see anything!" he declared.

"Perhaps Mack knows," Dennison suggested.

Three of the Blackwell's coachmen, including Mack, were volunteers with the neighborhood fire department, so Pierce lit out of the room on a dead run, hoping to hear some bit of news. For reasons beyond his understanding, he couldn't shake off the sensation that something was terribly wrong. It was more than the simple signal of the fire. Fires were commonplace things. Poorly built clapboard buildings and careless vagrants were well-known reasons for fires, not to mention those finer houses which went up when lamps were knocked over or fireplaces were left unattended. It was more than this and he had to know what it was that drove him to concern.

"Where's the fire?" he shouted, passing through the kitchen into the breezeway.

"Don't know," the cook answered in her brusque manner. "Nobody tells me anything."

Pierce felt the stinging cold bite at him through the thin material of his shirt. He went to the stable, refusing to turn back for a coat. "Where's the fire?" he asked again, this time to one of his remaining groomsmen.

"Lower end. Business district. They're calling out extra help because the Old Slip is up in flames and their department's hoses and pumps are frozen solid."

"The Old Slip? Are you certain?" Pierce's heart pounded in anticipation of the answer. Darlene and Abraham were less than two blocks up from the harbor and well within the Old Slip district.

"Aye, I'm certain. We had a rider come through afore the bells even sounded. Charlie and Mack grabbed up their gear and took off just as the signal came through. It's going to be a bad one."

"What about Ralph?" Pierce questioned, referring to the third Blackwell volunteer.

"He's in bed with a blow to the head. That new bay we bought got a bit out of control."

"Saddle my horse," Pierce said, ignoring the news about the injured man. "No, wait, a carriage! Get the landau ready and I'll drive it myself!" The groomsman stared at him in stunned silence. "Get to it, man! I'm going for my coat and I want it ready when I return. Oh, and throw in a stack of blankets."

Darlene! It was all he could think of. *Darlene and Abraham are in danger*!

He raced up the stairs, taking them two at a time. His father's concerned expression did nothing to slow him down. "It's the Old Slip," he called over his shoulder. "It's bad."

Nothing more needed to be said. Pierce knew that his father would understand his need to go. Dangers notwithstanding, Pierce had to find a way to get Darlene and Abraham to safety. His father would expect no less.

In his room he grabbed his frock coat and heavy woolen outer coat. Forgetting his top hat, he barely remembered to take his gloves and muffler.

"Bring them back here," his father said as he passed him in the hall.

"I will," Pierce replied and hurried off into the night. He had to find them. He had to save them. *Dear God, please don't let me be too late!*

sixteen

When thou passest through the waters, I will be with
thee; and through the rivers, they shall not overflow thee:
when thou walkest through the fire, thou shalt not be
burned; neither shall the flame kindle upon thee.
Isaiah 43:2

❧

After placing a kiss upon her sleeping father's forehead, Darlene secured her bonnet and did up the buttons of her coat. She felt a new peace and excitement that she couldn't put into words. She had accepted Jesus into her heart and the wonder of it consumed her. She felt giddy, almost like laughing out loud. What was it Pierce had told her? Something about having great joy in knowing a personal relationship with God. Was that why she felt so wonderful?

Grabbing up Esther's newly washed pot, Darlene hummed to herself, nearly skipping down the stairs. She felt so good! Her father had been very pleased with her choice and while she knew that pleasing him was important, it wasn't the reason she'd accepted Jesus as Messiah. No, God had done a work in her heart and she had come to Him in the full belief that there was more to life than laws and traditions.

She pulled the door to the shop closed and sniffed the air. There was a faint scent of wood smoke on the breeze, but on a night as cold as this, it wasn't unusual for the air to hang heavy with the smoke of coal and wood. She snuggled her face into the fur collar of her coat and hurried down the street to Esther's. She was already determined to share her new faith with Esther, even knowing that the old woman would call her a traitor and crazy. For reasons

141

beyond what Darlene could understand, however, she knew that she had to try to make Esther see what Christianity was all about. It wasn't leaving the Jewish faith behind. It was fulfilling it in the Messiah they had always known would come.

In the distance she could hear the clang of the fire bells. *How sad,* she thought, *that someone would suffer through the cold of the night while fire consumed their home or shop.* She instantly asked God to put out the blaze and keep the unknown folks from harm. New York seemed always to suffer with fires and Darlene couldn't help but wonder if Pierce's Chicago would be any different.

Pierce! The very thought of Pierce Blackwell caused her to tremble. Always before she'd been hesitant to dream of the words he'd told her. "I love you," he'd said and Darlene had pushed them aside knowing that a Jew could never marry a Christian. *But now we share faith in Christ,* she thought, and a smile broke across her painfully cold face. Just as quickly as it had come, however, it faded. *I'm still poor and unworthy of his social standing. Nothing can change that.*

She knocked on the door of Esther's tiny house and waited for some reply. After several minutes of stomping her boots to keep her feet from freezing, Darlene was happy to see the old woman peek from behind her curtained window.

"Hava!" Esther exclaimed, opening the door, "You should not have come out. The pot could wait until tomorrow."

"I know," Darlene said, coming into the house. She waited for Esther to close the door and take the pot before continuing. "I wanted to talk to you for a moment. I wanted to apologize for my attitude earlier."

Esther had just returned from her kitchen and the look upon her face was one of surprise. "You have changed your mind? You will live with me now?"

Darlene shook her head. "No, I didn't change my mind about that. Look," she hesitated, knowing that her words would not be well received. "I know you've worried about Tateh ever since he accepted the Christian Jesus as Messiah, but Esther, there are things you do not know. Things which I myself do not know, but am trying hard to understand. Tateh told me that Jesus didn't come to cancel out the laws of Moses, but to fulfill them. He said if we do the things Jesus commanded, we will still be keeping the laws."

"Feh!" Esther said indignantly. "Jesus commanded! What right does He have to command anything?"

"Because He's Messiah. He's God's Son and God sent Him into the world to save us from our sins!"

"Oy vey!" Esther said and pulled at her hair. "You haven't allowed such talk to fill your head, have you?"

Darlene smiled. "No, it's filled my heart. Oh, Esther, you must listen to me." She reached out and held the old woman's hand. "I know how hard this is for you. It was hard for me as well. I listened to the things Tateh said, I worried about his standing in the community and whether or not his friends would desert him, but God's peace is upon him. You don't understand and I'm not very good at explaining it. Tateh is very sick, but he's not afraid. God has given him great peace through Jesus. And He's given me the same peace."

Esther's face registered understanding. "Get out of my house. You and your father are dead to me from this moment on." She jerked her hand away and opened the door.

Darlene moved to the door, but turned back. "Please, Esther. We've been good friends all these years."

Her pleading fell on deaf ears. It was just as it might have been months ago had someone tried to talk to her about Jesus. No, that wasn't true. Because the words Pierce and her father had shared caused Darlene to think and ponder them over and over. She had been angry about them and rejected them as truth, but she always listened and later reflected. All she could do was hope that Esther would do likewise.

"I'll go, but I'll also pray for you."

The clang of fire bells suddenly grew louder and from somewhere in the darkness came shouts and screaming. Darlene looked up and even Esther came outside to see what might be the problem. Gazing up one way, Darlene saw nothing but the occasional glow of lamplight shining through the windows and a street lamp here and there. Turning, however, to look down the street from where she'd only come moments before, Darlene cried out, putting her hand to her mouth at the sight of bright orange and yellow flames. The wharves were on fire!

"Tateh!" Darlene rushed down the street, mindless of Esther's cries that she not go. Her father would be in danger and far too weak to move even if he was aware of the fire. She ran as fast as her legs would carry her, but the cold had made her stiff and with each step her feet felt like a million pins and needles were pricking them.

She was appalled to see the flames grow brighter. The fire was less than a half block from her shop. The heat was already warming her and thick black smoke was choking out her breath. A crowd had started to gather on the street and Darlene was startled when a policeman grabbed her.

"There, there. You can't be going in!" he declared.

"I have to. My father is in there." She pointed to the building, now only a block away.

"You can't go in. Leave the rescues to the fire department. Besides, I'm sure your papa will have seen the fire by now and made his way out."

"No, you don't understand. He's very sick." She wrenched away from him, but saw he wasn't about to let her pass. Just then a group of rowdies could be seen down the block breaking out the glass window of a shop and stealing what they could take.

The policeman called out for them to halt, and the distraction was enough to allow Darlene time to slip down the alley and make her way to the back door of the shop. Thick smoke poured down the alleyway as though it were being sucked through the narrow channels by some unseen force. Darlene buried her face in the fur of her collar and felt her way along the buildings. Stumbling over trash and other abandoned articles, Darlene finally reached the shop and turned the handle. The door didn't budge. It was locked!

"Of course it's locked," she muttered. She pushed up against it, but it refused to give. She ran at it, thrusting her shoulder against the door, but while it bowed ever-so-slightly, it wouldn't give in and only managed to cause Darlene a great deal of pain. She would have to gain entrance by going through the front, but how?

The smoke was most caustic now and she began to cough. Her eyes were burning fiercely and she knew there was no time to waste. She would go back to the front and if anyone tried to stop her, she would fight them any way she could.

Retracing her steps, Darlene found that the crowd had grown larger and that the policeman was now moving them even further up the street. He had been joined by three other members of his profession and no one seemed to notice Darlene as she slipped through the shadows and into the shop.

Panting, she slammed the door shut behind her. Inside, the smoke was not as bad, and with the light of the flames growing ever brighter, Darlene didn't even need a lamp to make her way up the stairs.

Still coughing, she choked out her father's name and hurried up the steps. She thought to grab some of their most precious articles and instantly reached up to take the *mezuzah* from the kitchen door. She tucked this into her coat pocket and for some reason thought of Pierce's valentine. She ran to her room, but just then a tremendous boom rattled the very floorboards beneath her feet. It sounded like a building collapsing, and instantly Darlene forgot about gathering up anything else and went to get her father. She had already formed a plan in her mind. She would help him from the bed and once they were downstairs and outside she would call those ever efficient policemen and get them to help her carry her father to safety.

"Tateh!" she exclaimed, hurrying into the room. "Tateh, there's a fire. It's got the entire Old Slip in flames. Come, we must hurry!" She pulled back the covers and went to get her father's coat.

Abraham remained silent and still. Darlene shook him hard. "Tateh, wake up."

And then, without waiting for any sign that he had heard her, Darlene suddenly knew that he was gone. "No!" she screamed into the smoky night air. "No!" She threw herself across his body and cradled him against her. "Don't die. Please don't die."

But it was too late. Abraham Lewy was dead.

The sound of bells and firemen mingled with breaking glass and the shouts of desperate people. There was no time for mourning, and though Darlene felt as though a part of her heart died with her father, self-preservation took over and she suddenly knew that she must hurry or perish in the fire.

Unable to consider leaving her father to be consumed by the flames, Darlene pulled his cover to the floor, then rolled his body off the bed and onto the cover. It wasn't an easy process, for even though her father had lost a great deal of weight, Darlene wasn't very big.

"Oh God," she prayed aloud, choking against the thickening smoke. "God, help me please. I believe You have watched over me this far. I believe you have taken Tateh to Your care, but I don't want to leave him here. Please help me!"

She struggled against the weight of her father and placed him in such a way that she could pull him along on the cover. How she would ever make it down the stairs without losing control of the body, she had no idea. But she was determined to try.

Pausing at the landing to draw her breath, Darlene screamed when hands reached out to close around her arm.

"It's me, Darlene."

"Pierce?"

"Yes, come on. I've got to get you to safety. Where's your father?"

"He's dead," she said, so matter-of-factly that it sounded unreal in her ears.

"Dead?"

"Yes, he's here on the floor. I have him on his cover and I was taking him out of the building." Her mind seemed unable to accept that Pierce had come. "Are you really here?" she asked suddenly.

Pierce laughed, but it was a very short, nervous laugh. "Yes, I'm really here. Now come on." He reached down and hoisted Abraham to his shoulder. "The building next door is already in flames. We'll have to hurry or we'll never get out in time." He coughed and gasped for air and this seemed to open Darlene's senses to the gravity of their situation.

"Hurry," she called over her shoulder, making her way down the stairs. She had just reached the bottom when the east wall of the shop burst into flames. It lit up the smoky room and instantly ate up the dry wood of the shelves.

"We'll have to go out the back way!" she yelled above the roar of the fire. Pierce nodded, and pushed her forward.

"Hurry up," he said. "Hurry or we'll die!"

Darlene pushed through the putrid smoke as if trying to cut a way through to the back room. There was no way to see in the smoke now, and suddenly she grew frightened wondering if Pierce was still behind her. There was no breath to be wasted on words, however, and all she could do was pray that God would allow them both to find their way.

Flailing her arms before her, Darlene finally hit the wall of the back room and then the door. She fumbled with the latch and slid back the lock. Pulling the door open only brought in more smoke and by now her head was growing light from the lack of oxygen. She felt dizzy and wondered if she could possibly make it another step. Slumping against the door frame, she was startled when Pierce pushed her through. He seemed to have the strength of ten men as he pulled her along the alleyway.

Hazy images filtered through Darlene's confusion. She knew they were in danger, but now, gasping for each breath, she couldn't imagine that anything mattered as much as fresh air. She wondered where they were going. Her mind played tricks on her and she became convinced that if she could just rest for a few moments, all would be well.

They had reached the front of the building and now the entire shop was in flames. Darlene still felt Pierce's iron-clad grip on her wrist, but her legs were growing leaden. She turned to see the walls of her home collapse and knew that the end of her world had come.

"My valentine!" she cried, suddenly trying to jerk away from Pierce.

"What?"

The air was only marginally better here, but Darlene felt her senses revitalized. "My valentine, the one you gave me!"

"I'll buy you a hundred others. You can't go back now; the place is completely destroyed." He pulled her along and made his way down the block to where he had hidden his buggy. *Thank you, God,* he offered in silent prayer. His one consuming worry had been that someone would find the landau and steal it for their own transportation.

Putting Abraham in the back, Pierce grabbed up several blankets and pulled Darlene to the driver's seat with him. He tucked blankets around them and then urged the nervous horses forward.

They made their way down the alley and side streets until they'd reached Wall Street. From here they could see the bright flames and eerie glow in the night sky, but the air was clean and only marginally scented with smoke.

"I don't even know if Esther made it out," Darlene suddenly murmured.

"But you're safe." Pierce put his arm around her shoulder and pulled her close. "I was so afraid I'd lose you."

Darlene looked up at him. The landau lantern swung lightly in the breeze making a play of sending out shadowy light to fall back and forth across their faces. "My father is dead." She said it as though Pierce could possibly have forgotten.

"I know," he answered. "I'm so very sorry, Darlene." He pulled her closer and wrapped his arms around her very tightly.

Crowds of people were lining the streets and as some went running to help with the fire, others were struggling to carry possessions to safety.

"The fire's comin' this-a-way!" a man yelled out and encouraged people to flee.

"Nothing will be left," Darlene said softly. She lay her face against the coarse wool of Pierce's coat. "I have nothing now."

"You have me," he whispered. "You've always had me."

seventeen

❧

Darlene's first waking moment was filled with panic. She had no idea where she was and the thought filled her with a consuming urgency. Sitting up abruptly, she looked around the room and found nothing that she could recognize. Early dawn light filtered through the gossamer-like curtains and gave the room only a hint of the day to come.

Flowered wallpaper lined the walls and a very soft mauve carpet touched her feet when Darlene got off the bed. She hurried to the window and was greeted with the stark reality of a cold winter's day. The neighborhood, an avenue lined with leafless trees and shrubs, was elegant even in this setting. Black wrought-iron fencing hemmed in the yard, and beyond this Darlene could make out the brick street.

Then the memories of the night before flooded back into her mind. The fire. Her father's death. Pierce. She sank to her knees on the carpeted floor and wept. Everything was gone. All lost in the fire. Her father had died, succumbing to consumption and now she was truly alone. She wrapped her arms around her and felt the soft folds of the nightgown. *It isn't even my gown,* she thought. The only thing left to her in the world were the clothes she'd worn out of the fire. And Pierce.

The last came as a tiny ember of thought. Pierce had said that she would always have him. But even that seemed lost and unlikely. How could he ever take her to be his wife? Especially now that she had nothing to offer him in the way of a dowry. The shop had burned to the ground, no doubt, and with it went every possible material article she could ever have offered a husband.

She cried even harder at this loss. Burying her face in her hands, she pulled her knees to her chest and thought of what she was going to do. It was all too much. She would have to bury her father, but even the idea of this caused her more misery than she could deal with. Who would perform the service? Her father was a Christian and would require a Christian burial, but she had no idea what that entailed. Who would prepare the body? The *hevra qaddish,* Jewish men from her community, would have normally prepared her father for burial and *Kaddish* would have been recited. Would anyone recite *Kaddish* over Abraham now? Would he have wanted them to? She was so confused.

Drying her eyes against the lacy edge of her sleeve, Darlene tried to remember if her father had ever made mention of such things.

Just then a light knock sounded upon the bedroom door. Getting to her feet, Darlene scrambled into the bed and pulled the covers high. "Come in," she called out and was surprised when Dennison Blackwell appeared.

"Are you up for a visitor?" he questioned.

She nodded, not really feeling like company, but knowing that this man had been her father's best friend in the world seemed to be reason enough to endure his visit.

He was dressed in a simple shirt and trousers. On his feet were slippers and a warm robe was tied loosely over his clothes to ward off the morning chill. "Forgive me for such an early visit, but I heard you crying and I felt compelled to come to offer you whatever comfort I could."

Darlene felt tears anew come to her eyes. "I tried very hard to be quiet," she said, snuffing back the tears.

"My dear, there is no need for that. Should you desire to cry down the very walls around you, you would be perfectly in your rights." He brought the vanity chair to her bedside and sat down wearily. "I am so very sorry about your father. He was my dearest friend and I will always feel the loss of his passing."

"He held you in very high regard," she replied, feeling the need to comfort him.

"And you?" Dennison said. "Are you going to be all right? Did you suffer any injuries during the fire?"

"I'm well," she said, feeling it was almost a lie. "I'm devastated by Tateh's death, but the fire did not harm me." *Other than to take everything I hold dear,* she thought silently.

"I thank God for that. When Pierce left here last night, all I could do was drop to my knees and pray. I feared for his safety, for yours and your father's, and I grieved for those I knew would be destroyed by the fire."

"I was so shocked when Pierce showed up that I could scarcely comprehend that he was really there. The smoke made my mind confused and incapable of clear thought and there was no way I could have carried Tateh to safety." She paused here, wiping away an escaping tear. "I couldn't let him be burned up in the flames. I knew he was already dead and I knew that he would be in Heaven with God." Dennison eyed her strangely for a moment, but she hurried on before he could speak. "I even knew that I would see him again, because he told me we would all be joined together in Heaven. But the pain of losing him and then the idea of leaving him to the fire, was just too much. I hope you don't think me terribly addle-brained."

"Not at all," Dennison murmured. His mind was clearly absorbed and this concerned Darlene.

"I don't know how to ask you this," she struggled for words. "I mean. . .well you see. . ."

"What is it, child?" he said, suddenly appearing not at all preoccupied. He reached out to pat her reassuringly. "You have only to name your request."

"It's my father's burial. You see, I have no idea what should take place, and I have no money. Everything was lost in the fire."

Dennison smiled. "You have nothing to worry about. I will see to everything and I insist on paying for the funeral myself. This will be one thing I can do in Abraham's memory and honor. I will see to it all." He paused, his face sobering. "But tell me, my dear, will you be grieved by the Christian service? Should I also plan for some type of service in your Jewish faith?"

Darlene shook her head. "I'm no longer of that faith. At least not like I was. Tateh said that Jesus is the fulfillment of our Jewish faith, but I'm still very new at this."

"Are you saying that you've accepted Jesus as your Savior?"

"Yes. Last night, before Tateh died. We talked and I felt such a peace. I know my friends would say that losing Tateh and everything I had on earth is my just punishment for forsaking the faith of my fathers, but I don't believe that. I don't know why, but I still have a peace inside that the fire didn't consume. Does that make sense?"

Dennison's face seemed filled with light. "It makes wonderful sense. I'm so very pleased to hear about your acceptance of Christ. Oh, Darlene, how happy your father must have been. He could die in blessed assurance of seeing you again in Heaven. It must have given him a great deal of peace."

"Yes, I believe it gave him the peace to die. At first, I was angry and very sad, but I lay here thinking last night that Tateh wouldn't want me to grieve. He would want me to trust God and not be angry that God took him from me."

"That's very wise coming from one so young."

Darlene swallowed hard and tried to smile. "I can't repay you for what you've done. At least, not yet. I don't know where I'll go or what I'll do. My Jewish friends will have nothing to do with me now that they know I believe in Jesus as Messiah."

"You've told them already?"

"I told Esther last night and that's as good as telling them all." This did make her smile and Dennison couldn't help but grin in a way that reminded her of Pierce. "They'll believe me to be a traitor and so I'll be an outcast."

"It won't be easy to face such a thing."

"Oh, I don't think I'll go back," Darlene said in a thoughtful way. "I don't know what I'll do just yet, but the old neighborhood is behind me now. I'm sure there's very little left after the fire, anyway."

"Well, that much is true. They're still trying to put out the flames. I'm afraid it burned all the way up to Wall Street and consumed most everything in its path."

Darlene nodded. "Somehow, I thought it would be that way." She squared her shoulders. "But God will provide, right?"

"Of course!" Dennison said and patted her hand again. "He already has. You are welcome to stay here for as long as you like. We've plenty of room and I know Pierce will be very happy to have your company here."

Darlene felt her cheeks grow warm. "I'm very thankful he came to us last night."

"As am I. Does he know about your new faith?"

Darlene shook her head. "No. There was no time to speak of such things and all I could really think about was Tateh being dead."

"He's going to be delighted," Dennison said with a huge smile. "I think it will be an answer to his many prayers concerning you."

"Concerning me?"

"You sound surprised. Surely you know he has deep feelings for you."

Her face grew even hotter. How could she explain that Pierce's feelings couldn't possibly be as strong as her own? Then, too, how could she speak to this man, his father, of the love she felt for his son? The Blackwells were rich and quite esteemed in society; surely Dennison Blackwell would not want to hear of her love.

"I see I've embarrassed you. Not to worry, I won't say another word. But, you should tell Pierce of your acceptance of Jesus at the first possible moment. It will probably answer a great many questions for you." With these mystic words he rose to his feet. "I will leave you to rest. You are not to get up from that bed for at least two days. Doctor's orders."

"What doctor?" Darlene questioned in confusion.

Dennison shrugged. "Doctor Blackwell," he said with a laugh. "A poor excuse for a physician if ever there was one, but nevertheless, I insist. I may not be a doctor, but I know that you've endured far too much for your own good. Two days of bed rest and pampering and you'll feel like a new person."

"Mr. Blackwell?"

"Yes?"

"Thank you for being so kind. You and Pierce have both been so generous. I know that my father came to an understanding of Jesus through you."

"You are most welcome, my dear."

"Would you extend my thanks to Pierce? Tell him that his prayers were answered."

Dennison looked confused. "You want me to tell him that you have found Jesus for yourself? Don't you want to wait and tell him yourself?"

"I think he will take great peace of mind from it and since he's partially responsible, I think he should know as soon as possible. Do you mind?" she asked, suddenly concerned that she'd expected too much.

"Not at all," he said in a fatherly way that implied great pride. "It shall be my honor."

He left her with that, and Darlene relaxed back against the pillows. Her heart felt much lighter for the sharing of her concerns. Mr. Blackwell said that she could remain in his home for as long as she liked. This gave her great comfort, and that he would tell Pierce that Darlene was now a Christian. She yawned and snuggled down into the warmth of the bed. She tried to imagine Pierce's reaction, but before she could consider anything else, her eyelids grew very heavy and finally closed in sleep.

Several hours later, Darlene awoke to the sound of someone puttering around her room. Groggily opening her eyes and forcing herself to sit up, she found a young woman in a starched white apron and high-collared black work dress standing at the foot of her bed.

"Good morning, ma'am. I'm Bridgett. I've brought your breakfast. Mr. Blackwell said to remind you that you're not to set foot out of the bed, except for the hot bath I'm to draw for you after you eat."

A hot bath? Darlene thought. But Tateh had only died the night before! Did these *goyim* have no sense of propriety? How could she indulge in such comforts during the mourning period? Then it suddenly hit her. Perhaps bathing in such circumstances was a Christian tradition. *Oy vey!* but there was so much to learn.

Darlene smiled weakly. Bridgett's immaculately ordered red hair caused her to smooth back her own tangled curls. "I'm a frightful mess," she declared.

Bridgett made no comment, but instead brought Darlene breakfast on a lovely white wicker bed tray. Poached eggs, toast and jam, and three strips of bacon were neatly arranged on a delicately patterned china plate. Beside this was an ornate set of silverware, a linen napkin, and a steaming cup of tea.

"Thank you," she said, but the girl only bobbed a curtsey and took herself off through a side door.

Darlene looked at the breakfast and almost laughed out loud at the bacon. *Oy vey!* but what would Esther say? She wondered how it was with Christians and how she would ever learn the right and wrong thing to do. Were there things which Christians didn't eat? Studying the plate a moment longer, Darlene decided against the bacon.

The toast and jam were safe enough and it was this that she immediately began to eat on. Gone was the headache of the night before and the only reminder was the heavy smell of smoke on her body and in her hair.

When the maid returned, Darlene had finished her tea and toast and set the tray aside.

"The bath is in here, ma'am."

Darlene stared after Bridgett and finally followed her. She found herself in a charmingly arranged room. A huge tub of steaming water awaited her and beside it was a tray with a variety of bath salts and scented soaps. On the other side stood a lovely vanity with so many lotions and powders that Darlene couldn't imagine ever using them all.

"I'll take your gown, ma'am," Bridgett said, obviously waiting for Darlene to disrobe.

Feeling rather self-conscious, both because of the stranger and the finery around her, Darlene hesitated. Thinking of the *mikveh,* the ritual bath used by Jewish women for cleansing before marriage, and after childbirth or menstruation, Darlene no longer felt shy. The *mikveh* required that her body be inspected before immersion and therefore it was far more personal. Bridgett merely wanted to take the gown away and leave her to privacy of her bath.

"Do your people bathe during times of mourning?" Darlene asked hesitantly.

Bridgett's expression contorted. "My people?"

Darlene twisted her hands anxiously and rephrased her question. "Do Christians take baths. . .well, that is to say . . .is it all right to take a bath after a loved one has died?"

Bridgett looked at her strangely for a moment. "They take a bath whenever it suits them. Cleanliness is next to godliness or so my mother says."

Darlene nodded, feeling torn between old traditions and new. Well, she'd put aside the bacon, so perhaps accepting the bath wasn't too bad. After all, Bridgett said it was perfectly acceptable. Slipping out of the gown, she handed it to the maid and stepped into the tub.

Darlene sank into the hot water with a grateful smile on her face. She let the water come over her shoulders and finally dipped her head below and enjoyed the sensation of warmth. She was at peace and her heart, though heavy for the passing of her father, was not worried. She allowed her mind to think of Abraham and of the happiness he'd had in knowing that she'd found Jesus. It was the most important decision she could ever make, he'd told her once. And now she knew for herself that it was.

After her bath, Bridgett reappeared with a fresh gown of soft pink lawn and a robe to match. After helping Darlene dress, Bridgett took her to a chair beside the fireplace and proceeded to dry her long wet hair. Darlene had never known such care and thoroughly enjoyed the pampering. It wasn't long before Bridgett had the long, tangled mess dry and brushed to a shining, orderly fashion. They agreed to leave it down before Bridgett led Darlene back to bed where fresh linens and covers replaced the smoke scented ones from the night before.

She'd barely gotten back into bed when the door was flung open and Eugenia Blackwell swept into the room.

"That's enough, Bridgett. You may go," she said in her haughty, superior way.

Bridgett bobbed again and hurried from the room, taking Darlene's towels with her. Eugenia frowned at her for a moment, leaving Darlene to feel rather intimidated. She thought perhaps she should say something, but couldn't imagine what it might be.

"Well, I see you have composed yourself," Eugenia said, staring down at Darlene.

"Yes, you've all been very kind to help me." *There,* thought Darlene. *I've said something complimentary and surely she'll realize I only mean to be a congenial guest.*

"Yes, of course. But then, what else could we do? It wasn't as if we had a choice."

Darlene frowned. "Mr. Blackwell assured me it was no trouble."

"But he would say that, my dear. That's how it is done in proper society."

Darlene cringed inside at the coldness in her voice. It was clearly evident that Eugenia did not share her brother's hospitality towards Darlene.

"May I be frank with you?" Eugenia suddenly asked.

This surprised Darlene who thought Eugenia had done quite a complete job of that up till now, without seeking anything closely resembling permission. "Of course," she finally managed to say.

Eugenia took up the chair vacated earlier by her brother. Sitting across from Darlene, she maintained her rigid, austere posture and frowned. "You must understand that what I am about to say should remain strictly confidential." Darlene nodded and Eugenia continued. "I am, of course, quite sorry to learn of your father's death. However, your presence in this house creates a bit of a problem for us. I find my nephew easily confused by you and because of this he has begun to question the things that should matter most in his life."

"I don't know what you're talking about," Darlene said

in complete confusion.

"But I'm sure you do," she replied rather snidely. "Pierce fancies himself in love with you. Whether or not he's mentioned this to you is of little concern to me. Eventually he will come to his senses and you will be forgotten. Pierce will marry Amanda Ralston, a woman chosen for him by his father and myself. Amanda is of a proper New York family and can offer Pierce much by their marriage." Darlene felt as though Eugenia had actually struck her a blow. "You, my dear, simply cannot be so heartless as to want Pierce to give up the things which make him happiest."

"Certainly not."

Eugenia smiled rather stiffly. "I'm glad to hear you say it. Therefore, you will understand when I say, also, that you cannot remain in this house. Pierce will continue to be confused by you and I'm afraid that if you remain, his father will have no other choice but to cut him off entirely. This would be a grave tragedy."

"But, I thought, well. . ." Darlene fell silent. She wasn't about to try to explain her thoughts to Eugenia Blackwell Morgan. The woman obviously could not care less that her words had pierced Darlene through to the soul.

"The kindest thing you can do is to leave as soon as possible. Don't make a scene and don't even say goodbye. I will give you assistance in reaching whatever destination you like."

"But I have no one now and Mr. Blackwell is arranging my father's funeral. I certainly can't just walk away from that."

"I suppose you are right," Eugenia said, as if only considering this for the first time. "After the funeral then. I will come to you and supply you with the proper funds. You can take yourself to a hotel until you find somewhere to board permanently." She got to her feet, acting as though the matter was entirely resolved. "You can only mean disaster to Pierce, and if you care at all about his well-being, you will go as soon as possible and give him nothing more to dwell on."

Darlene wanted to scream at her to mind her own business, but frankly the shock of Eugenia's forward nature was more than enough to silence her. She was still staring at the chair Eugenia had just vacated when a loud knock on her bedroom door signaled yet another visitor.

"Come in."

Pierce burst through the door with a huge smile on his face. "Father just told me your news. Darlene, I'm overwhelmed." He paused for a moment as though stricken by her appearance. "You are so beautiful!" he declared.

Darlene tried to smile, but Eugenia's words came back to haunt her. Perhaps she was bad for Pierce and perhaps her love for him would spell disaster if left unchecked.

Pierce crossed the room and took hold of her hands. Raising each one to his lips he kissed first one and then the other. "I'm very happy that you've accepted Jesus as your Savior. I can't begin to tell you how I've prayed for this very thing."

"I know," she whispered. "I remember you said you would pray for me to know the truth. Before Tateh died, he helped me see that truth for myself."

Pierce pulled up the chair so that it touched the side of the bed. "I can't tell you how sorry I am that he's gone. I wanted so much for you and your father to come west with me. I even secured a physician to travel with us. He's a man of your own people who also believes in Jesus."

The idea that Pierce would do this for her father deeply touched Darlene. "How very kind."

"I suppose I had my motives," he grinned. "I wanted to leave no stone unturned, so to speak. I wanted there to be no arguments, nothing which would stand in the way of your coming along. Now that he's dead, I realize you will feel his loss very profoundly, but I know too that you need to make decisions about your own future. A future I hope will include me."

Darlene lowered her face and looked at her hands. Eugenia's cold eyes and haughty stare seemed to be all that she could think of.

"I know this is a bit overwhelming, and I won't say another word on the matter until after the funeral. I just want you to have heart and be assured that you needn't worry for tomorrow." He leaned over and surprised her by kissing her gently on the cheek. "I still love you."

He left without expecting any reply and Darlene could feel her cheek burning where his lips had touched it. *He loves me, but I'm no good for him.* She fell back against the pillows and at once wished more than ever that her father could be there to advise her. *Pray,* an inner voice seemed to whisper. *Pray to your Heavenly Father and He will advise you.* This thought gave her peace. Perhaps God would show her what to do.

eighteen

*And the Lord God said, It is not good that the man should
be alone; I will make him an help meet for him.*
Genesis 2:18

᠕

Darlene reflected on her father's funeral in the silence of
her bedroom. The Christian funeral had been quiet and simple and very comforting. The minister had spoken of a day
when all things would be passed away and the resurrection
of those in Christ Jesus would take place. She tried to imagine what a reunion it would be and how very happy her
father would be to see her again, and how he wouldn't be
sad or sick.

She looked down at her sober gray gown. Eugenia had
insisted that black would be more appropriate, but this
was a dress borrowed from Constance and Darlene didn't
want anyone to go to the expense of dying it black and
making it unusable to the young girl again.

"Borrowed clothes and somebody else's room," she muttered to the walls, "that's all I have left." Well, that wasn't
entirely true. Dennison had told her of a small insurance
policy that her father had taken on the shop. It seemed that
the policy was protection against fires and would allow, in
cases of complete destruction, a small amount of money
for rebuilding. He had promised to see to the situation in a
few days and to take care of all the necessary paperwork.
Darlene was relieved, even if it only amounted to several
hundred dollars. It would give her enough money to take
care of herself for a while and it would allow her more
freedom to decide her future.

She went to the window and stared out on the false spring day. For all appearances it would seem spring was just around the corner, but she knew better. They all did. Sometimes fair weather came in the middle of winter, just like this. It would lull you into a false sense of security and then render you helpless in a blizzard or ice storm. Maybe that's what she was allowing to happen to her in regards to the insurance money. Was she being lulled into a false sense of security by placing her values in monetary needs? Tateh had said, "God will provide." And of course, He always did. So why should she fret so now, and seek all manner of solutions, all of which had nothing to do with God?

"Oh God," she whispered the prayer, "I'm afraid and I don't know very much about how to follow Jesus. I need help and I don't know where else to turn, but to You. You've always been there and Tateh said You were the same God of my childhood, that You are now of my adulthood. Tateh said You would never fail and never desert me and that I could come to You with all of my hopes and fears and You would take care of my needs." She saw the empty branches of the trees rustle slightly in the breeze. "I need You, God. I need to know what I must do and where I should go. I love Pierce so much, but I know that his aunt is right. I can never be the wife he needs. Please help me."

She felt so torn apart. Tateh was gone and Pierce soon would be. She had no idea where to go or what to do, and she wanted so much to please God and be brave.

"I'll never be good enough," she said with a sigh, and then the words of the minister came to mind. At Abraham's funeral, he had said that no one was saved because they were good enough. He said they were saved by grace and that one need only have faith in that grace in order to find their way to God.

"I can have faith," she whispered and the words gave her heart strength. "I can have faith. I might have no answers and very little money, but faith is the one thing I can surely dig up from within." She smiled and knew that if Tateh were here, he'd be quite pleased with her.

The door to her room opened abruptly and Darlene knew without turning around that it would be Eugenia. She was the only one bold enough to simply enter the room without knocking.

"I see you haven't yet changed back into your own clothes," Eugenia announced. "Well, I suppose there is still time."

Darlene looked at her, but said nothing.

"I've brought you enough money to keep yourself in decent style until you can find a job or other friends to take you in." Eugenia tossed a small cloth bag onto the bed.

"I don't want your money, Mrs. Morgan."

"Nonsense. You will take it and I will have the carriage ready to take you wherever you might instruct him to go. I think it would be best if you were to make your departure before the evening meal. Any delay you make will only create further problems."

"But Mr. Blackwell is handling my affairs and. . ."

"You are no good for this family and even worse for Pierce."

"I would disagree with you, Madam," Pierce said, entering the open door without warning. "I believe quite the contrary. Miss Lewy is excellent for me and I intend to see that she never gets away from me. Now, stop interfering and leave us to talk."

Eugenia was stunned by his comeuppance. "How dare you speak to me like that?"

Pierce put a protective arm around Darlene's shoulders. "You've stuck your nose into my business one too many times, Aunt. Father and I have already discussed Darlene's future and I have great plans for her."

"But this is nonsense," Eugenia stated firmly. "You must

marry of woman a means and one with a social bearing that matches your own. You cannot dally with this little Jewess and expect your future to know anything but heartache. I have already spoken with Amanda and she assures me that she'll take you back, no questions asked."

"As I said earlier," Pierce replied, his voice rather cold and unemotional, "you are interfering where no one wants you and I won't tolerate your attitude towards Darlene any longer. Either see your way fit to treat her with respect, or leave." He dropped his hold on Darlene and stepped forward as if to create a barrier between Darlene and his aunt.

"Well!" Eugenia declared and left without another word.

Pierce turned. "It seems I am ever saving you from runaway freighters or burning buildings or destructive old women," he said with a smile. "I'm sorry for Eugenia's attitude. I promise you that she doesn't speak for me or for my family."

Darlene sobered a bit. "She's right though. I don't fit into your world."

Pierce laughed. "So what? I don't fit into my world. I despise the rhetoric and snobbery. I've long planned to leave it, as you well know. There's only been one thing stopping me."

"What?"

"You," he said softly.

Darlene looked up into his face and felt her protests melt away. His dark eyes seemed to drink her in and his face beckoned her touch. Denying herself no longer, Darlene reached a hand to his cheek and found his hand quickly covering hers to hold it in place.

"I love you," he said.

Darlene knew her moment of truth had come. She lowered her gaze. "I love you," she whispered in a barely audible tone.

"What was that?" He lifted her chin with his free hand.

His eyes sparkled with amusement. "I couldn't quite hear you."

"I love you," she stated quite frankly. "Although I've tried not to."

"But why?" He sounded almost hurt.

Darlene shook her head. "Right now, I can't think of one reason."

"I'm serious. If there's something I should know. . ."

She put her finger to his lips and felt a current of excitement coarse through her. "I thought you should marry someone of your own standing. I can never serve proper teas in proper parlors and I will never be accepted by your society friends. To them a Jew is a Jew is a Jew, whether he believes in Jesus or not."

Pierce pulled her tightly into his arms. "I'm not marrying my society friends, nor do I care one whit what they think. God knows our hearts, Darlene. He has brought us together and brought you to an understanding of His Son Jesus. Do you suppose He would desert us now?"

Darlene melted against him, feeling such a strange sensation of emotion. She truly did love him, but she loved him enough that she couldn't bear the thought of saddling him with an improper wife. "But what of Chicago?"

"What of it? I plan to go there and build us a new life. I will build you the finest house ever seen that far west and people will come from miles around and say, 'Look what that man did out of love for his wife!' "

"Oh, Pierce, be serious."

"I am. I want to spend the rest of my life showing you just how serious I am," he said in a low husky tone that put goosebumps on Darlene's arms. "I want you for my wife. I've wanted it since last year when I came for my Valentine's suit. Remember?"

"I couldn't forget. I lost my valentine in the fire," she said sadly. "It was quite precious to me because I knew, even though you'd not signed it, that it was from you."

"Marry me," Pierce whispered against her ear. He kissed her lightly upon her hair, then her cheek, and finally her lips. Hovering there, he whispered again. "Marry me and be my Valentine forever."

"But. . ."

He silenced her with his lips in a passionate kiss and when he pulled away, Darlene smiled. "I suppose I should give in on your ability to kiss alone, but I won't." Pierce frowned and she continued. "You must consider that people in Chicago might well not like you being married to a Jewess. You have to think about this because it might well ruin your reputation and end your prosperity. *Di libe iz zis —nor zi iz gut mit broyt.*"

"And what's that supposed to mean?"

"Love is sweet—but it's better with bread. In other words, love won't put bread on the table and it won't fill your belly when you're hungry. If people in Chicago should act harshly towards you because of me, it won't matter how much we love each other."

"Nonsense," Pierce said, holding her close. "You will be Mrs. Pierce Blackwell and your beauty and graciousness will win them all over. Now, stop putting me off and say yes."

Darlene grinned and nodded with a sigh. "Yes." It seemed so right and in her heart she knew that God had answered the prayer she'd pleaded only moments before.

epilogue

I will bless the Lord at all times: his praise shall
continually be in my mouth. Psalm 34:1

ॐ

Darlene flushed at the passionate kiss Pierce placed upon
her lips. The minister cleared his throat and both Dennison
and Constance Blackwell could be heard to chuckle. When
he pulled away, Darlene shook her head and smiled.

"I present the happy couple, Mr. and Mrs. Pierce Blackwell," the minister announced.

"Oh, Pierce!" Constance said, coming to hug her big
brother. "I'm so happy for you! How wonderful to get married on Valentine's Day!"

"He only did that so he could avoid going to the bachelor
ball again," Dennison teased then added, "My dear, you are
a radiant bride. Welcome to our family." He kissed her
lightly on the cheek and hugged her gently.

"Thank you," Darlene whispered. "Thank you for everything."

Eugenia Blackwell Morgan's absence from the wedding
did nothing to spoil the fun. The house staff laid out a
wonderful wedding breakfast and everyone gorged themselves until they could hold no more. Pierce had worried
that Darlene would regret such a small wedding, but she
assured him over and over that it was only important that
he be there, whether the rest of the world showed up or
not.

When evening came and the couple made their way to
the privacy of their first bedroom as man and wife, Darlene
felt an uneasy nervous flutter in her stomach and trembled
when Pierce lifted her to carry her across the threshold.

"I love you," he said, gently putting her down again. "I will always love only you."

Darlene's nerves instantly settled. She stared up into the face of her husband and smiled. "And I love you and so long as I live, you'll be my only Valentine."

"That reminds me," Pierce said. He went to the large bureau and pulled open a drawer. Fishing out an envelope he brought it to her and grinned. "Happy Valentine's Day."

"But I didn't get you anything," she protested.

He nuzzled her neck with a kiss. "I'm sure we'll work that out."

She blushed, feeling her face grow hot. Concentrating on opening the card, she found it to be an identical replica of the one she'd lost in the fire. But this time it was signed as well.

"To Darlene, my darling wife, with all my love, Pierce," she read and tears came instantly to her eyes. She looked up at him and saw the tenderness in his expression and knew that God had done a wonderful thing in her life. Stepping into his arms once again, she thought of the future and the hope that lay before them. It was good to know that they would face it together. It was good to know they'd have God to guide their way.

"Thank you for my Valentine," she said, pulling away. "I'll cherish it always." She turned to place it on the bureau, but Pierce reached out and pulled her back with a deep, mischievous laugh.

"I'm not letting you get away," he said, then grinning in a roguish manner, he pulled loose the ribbon from her hair and whispered, "Now, about my Valentine. . ."

A Letter To Our Readers

Dear Reader:

In order that we might better contribute to your reading enjoyment, we would appreciate your taking a few minutes to respond to the following questions. When completed, please return to the following:

Rebecca Germany, Managing Editor
Heartsong Presents
P.O. Box 719
Uhrichsville, Ohio 44683

1. Did you enjoy reading *My Valentine*?
   ❑ Very much. I would like to see more books
   by this author!
   ❑ Moderately
   I would have enjoyed it more if _____

   _____

2. Are you a member of **Heartsong Presents**? ❑Yes ❑No
   If no, where did you purchase this book? _____

   _____

3. What influenced your decision to purchase this
   book? (Check those that apply.)

   ❑ Cover   ❑ Back cover copy

   ❑ Title   ❑ Friends

   ❑ Publicity   ❑ Other_____

4. How would you rate, on a scale from 1 (poor) to 5
   (superior), the cover design? _____

5. On a scale from 1 (poor) to 10 (superior), please rate the following elements.

___Heroine   ___Plot

___Hero   ___Inspirational theme

___Setting   ___Secondary characters

6. What settings would you like to see covered in **Heartsong Presents** books?_____

_____

_____

7. What are some inspirational themes you would like to see treated in future books?_____

_____

_____

8. Would you be interested in reading other **Heartsong Presents** titles?   ❏ Yes   ❏ No

9. Please check your age range:
   ❏ Under 18   ❏ 18-24   ❏ 25-34
   ❏ 35-45   ❏ 46-55   ❏ Over 55

10. How many hours per week do you read? _____

Name _____

Occupation _____

Address _____

City_____ State_____ Zip _____

101 Ways to Say "*I Love You*"

How do you say I love you? By sending love notes via overnight delivery. . .by watching the sunrise together. . . by calling in "well" and spending the day together. . .by sharing a candlelight dinner on the beach. . .by praying for the man or woman God has chosen just for you.

When you've found *the one*, you can't do without *one hundred and one ways* to tell them exactly how you feel. Priced to be the perfect subsitute for a birthday card or love note, this book fits neatly into a regular envelope. Buy a bunch and start giving today!

Specially Priced!
Buy 10 for only $9.97!
or 5 for only $4.97!

48 pages, Paperbound, 3½" x 5½"

······Heart♥ng ······

HEARTSONG PRESENTS TITLES AVAILABLE NOW:

·······Presents·······